BABY BLUE

(A JACK MCCOUL CAPER BOOK 3)

DWIGHT HOLING

Baby Blue
(A Jack McCoul Caper)
Alternate Print Edition
Copyright 2016 by Dwight Holing
Published by Jackdaw Press
All Rights Reserved

ISBN: 978-1-7347404-4-8

For More Information, please visit dwightholing.com.

See how you can **Get a Free Book** at the end of this novel.

For Mark Swope

J ack McCoul was nursing a cup of coffee in San Francisco General Hospital's cafeteria when he caught a waft of something feral. It reminded him of an opossum he spooked in a Chinatown alley the night before. The startled creature hissed like a tire losing air, flopped on its side, and foamed at the mouth. Uncorking a roadkill reek was the final act. The scared-to-death performance did the trick and Jack backed away quick, yet another lesson that even con artists could be conned.

Now it was a man wrapped in the cocoon of a ripe blanket. He sidled up to the table and said, "You gonna finish that?"

Jack pushed the lukewarm brew toward him. "Help yourself."

The man snatched the prize and penguin-walked across the linoleum to the tune of one sole flapping. He stopped at the condiments counter and poured in several packets of sugar while keeping a lookout for other scavengers prowling for freebies.

A long-awaited El Niño was dumping rain and forcing a nearby homeless encampment inside. The hospital maintained an open-door policy and no one was ever turned away for lack of money, insurance, or a bath. It was a rare night when any of the 600 beds went empty, including those in the psych unit and the locked wards for sick inmates who'd been hauled over from the Hall of Justice. The ER was the busiest place of all, its reputation as the original knife and gun club hard earned and well deserved.

Jack held no fondness for the century-old hospital even though it was his birthplace. His mother had spent torturous days and hellish nights in the cancer ward before checking herself out so she could die in her own bed. His father had been rushed to the burn unit after his fellow firefighters had pulled him from a Noe Valley four-alarmer; they'd been too late before they'd even hit the lights and siren. Jack was only there to kill time until visiting hours began. He checked his watch and started to stand when fingertips brushed the nape of his neck and a voice that used to call his name from across a pillow sat him back down.

"Hello, Jack. How long has it been?"

The raven hair was shorter but the legs still impossibly long. The blue eyes hadn't lost any of their sparkle either. It was Grace Millefiori, all right—all beauty and all trouble all rolled into one.

Jack masked his surprise by flashing grin and grimace. "Three years, four months, six days, but who's counting? You remember Prague and the bent banker we took down. You were the one who pulled a double switch and ran off with the score, and I was the one left standing in Wenceslas Square holding the bag. Stacks of cut up French *Vogue*, no less." He gave it a couple of beats. "So much for honor among thieves."

Grace did that thing with her lips she'd always done before speaking—the way Italians air-kissed upon meeting. She was born and raised in the shadow of Coit Tower, but like many who grew up in the Little Italy neighborhood, her old country roots ran deep.

"Honor is based on trust and I trusted you'd get away." Her fingertips traced his jaw line. "I trusted you would know I didn't have a choice. And most of all I trusted you would forgive me." Her eyes leveled on his. "I still do."

Grace leaned in close and her dusky whisper kissed his face. Wingbeats he used to call it. That's what he always told her it felt like—a dove flying close by. "Was I wrong?"

Jack wadded a paper napkin and started playing a shell game using his palms as cups. "I haven't thought about it."

"Sure you have."

He kept sliding the wadded napkin, his hands as quiet as ever. "Where did you go?"

Grace Millefiori's head tilted. "South America. Argentina, mostly."

"And about why you trusted I'd understand? You know, running off with *our* money."

"That's a long story and I don't have time right now. I'm on my way to visit someone."

"Do you still live down there?" Jack asked in a tone reserved for weather inquiries. She signaled no. "Move back to your old neighborhood?" Again, casual.

Her hair moved in a dark and silent wave. "The Central Valley is home now. A vineyard, actually. We grow grapes and make wine." She breathed in, breathed out. More wingbeats. "My husband and I do. He's the reason I'm here. He had surgery."

Jack knew he was supposed to say something hopeful about her husband's condition. He asked his name instead.

"You wouldn't know him," she said.

"Try me."

"Stefan Fabro."

"As in Fabro wines?"

"Yes."

"Old chug-a-jug. That's what we called it back in high school. You could get a screw top of hearty burgundy for $4.99. Anybody in the Mission would buy it for you if you gave them a swallow."

"I see you haven't lost any of your charm."

Jack shuffled the wadded napkin a few more times. "You married well. The Fabro family pioneered California winemaking. They're one of the biggest grape growers in the state."

"The industry has changed a lot since Stefan's great-grandfather founded the company. Tastes have changed." She paused. "A lot of things have changed."

He quit sliding his palms. "Meaning you didn't exactly tell your in-laws about your—how shall I put it—colorful past?"

Her lips were umber, the color of Tuscan earth. They turned at the corners into what could be a frown or a smile. "And what about you? Still up to your old tricks or have you settled down?"

"I'm married too, if that's what you're asking. I sold a start-up, own a little commercial real estate in the Mission, watch what I eat, and exercise regularly."

"Your wife's a lucky woman." Grace's eyelashes sent the equivalent of a flock of birds fluttering his way. "We've always been traveling the same path, you and I. It seems we still are."

"I doubt it." He lifted his palms and turned them up for show. The napkin was gone.

"You're a confidence man, Jack. Doubt has never been your thing." She leaned in close and kissed him. And then she was like the napkin too.

～

THE ELEVATOR WAS TOO DAMN small and too damn slow. Jack

stared at the flashing numbers but instead of seeing a light blink with each new floor, he saw alternating faces. First Grace's and then his wife Katie's and then Grace's again. When the doors swished open, he was a bull charging out of a chute.

"Whoa, partner," boomed a deep voice. "This is a hospital."

The nurse's bouffant was the color and texture of cotton candy. Her eyebrows were waxed and her makeup heavy. She was six foot three if she was an inch. The stitched name tag on her cranberry scrubs spelled out *Taylor S.*

"Sorry. The ICU. It's on this floor, right?"

Three colored pens attached to a braided lanyard hung midway between her Adam's apple and chest. Blue, red, and green. "You need a special pass to visit patients here."

He dug in his pocket and pulled out a slip of yellow paper.

Taylor S.'s fingernails were lacquered to a high gloss. The knuckles were those of a boxer. "You sign this yourself?"

Jack didn't blink. "What makes you say that?"

"I can actually read the name, that's why." Her grin was sly.

"The clerk in Admitting reminded me of my English teacher at Saint Joe's. Sister Mary Ascension. Had a thing for penmanship and wielded a wicked ruler if your down strokes weren't parallel." Jack shook his fingers as if stung. "I never could get the cursive capital *Q* right. Always looked like a 2. Know what I mean?"

The nurse scrawled something across the yellow slip with the green pen. "Here you go, handsome."

"Thanks, Nurse..."—he chinned at the name tag—"S, what, as in Swift?"

"Strangelove." Her laugh was killer. "Come on, follow me."

They made their way down the hall to a room that resembled an airport flight control center. Laptops crowded desks that were circled like wagons. Lights flashed from multiple screens. Digitized lines carved staircases on heart monitoring machines.

The chilly air was punctuated by beeps and the occasional scream of an alarm. The room oversaw glass-walled isolation rooms and open wards crammed with beds. All were full. Drip lines dangled from IVs the way shroud-lines hung from parachutes.

"Now, who is it you want to see?" Her fingers poised over a keyboard.

"Henri LeConte," Jack said.

"You say it like he's French. I'm a big New Wave fan myself. Godard. Truffaut. Louis Malle. I especially admire the actresses." She mimed patting her bouffant. "Bridget Bardot's my idol but how about that Jacqueline Bisset? When people ask her how to pronounce her name she juts out her ass and says 'Rhymes with kiss it.' " Her heh-heh-heh was more roar than purr. "Does that mean your friend spells it with an *i*? Found him. Cardiac Care. He was admitted two days ago."

"I only got word a couple of hours ago."

"Are you family, priest, or lawyer?"

The old grifter was Jack's mentor. Both were supposedly retired from the game—Henri because of age, Jack because of a promise he made to Katie.

"Family," he said automatically.

Taylor S. read the yellow slip again. "Isn't McCoul Irish?"

"Henri's my uncle on my mother's side, don't you know?"

She chuckled at the sudden brogue. "I bet you're a party on St. Paddy's Day."

Jack gestured at the beds on the other side of the glass. "Which one's his?"

"Follow me." She grabbed a tablet off the desk and swiped open the screen. Her size 13 clogs clopped as loudly as a Clydesdale pulling a beer wagon.

Jack made a career out of being able to control his emotions —keeping steely nerved when needed, showing panic when a scam called for it—but seeing Henri flat out in a hospital bed tested his resolve. A ventilator took the place of the usual silk ascot. The trademark pencil-thin moustache was lost among the weeds of white stubble.

"Can't he get a shave at least?"

"He's on Coumadin. We can't risk a nick. If it were up to me, I'd touch up his cheeks with blush but what if he's allergic?" Her bouffant waggled. "We can't risk an infection either."

An IV needle poked the top of Henri's hand. The tape holding it in place was see-through. The veins beneath resembled squid ink linguini. Jack placed his hand on his friend's wrist.

"Has he woken up?"

The nurse's expression signaled no.

"Is he in any pain?"

Taylor S. read from her tablet. "He was unconscious when admitted. Cardiac arrest. EMT started CPR and administered external defib en route. A trauma team took over once they got him in the ER. Let's see, meds included lignocaine, magnesium, and atropine. After the third shock, they gave him 300 mikes of amiodarone." Her nose wrinkled. "Ooh. That stuff is nasty."

"Why didn't they take him to Marin County General? He lives in Sausalito."

She studied the tablet again. "Because the 911 was here in the city."

Jack checked his surprise. "Does it say where?"

"The chart only gives the time and closest intersection. He was picked up in the Financial District. The corner of Sansome and California."

"What about surgery?"

Taylor S. read some more. "I'm sorry, handsome. It's contraindicated." She made a frown. "You want a minute alone with him? I'll be at my station. Make sure you stop by and say hi on your way out."

Jack kept his fingers on Henri's wrist. The pulse was faint but there. A loop of memories played. Henri's specialty was forgery scams involving fine arts, antiquities, and historic documents. Jack could see the first play they ever made together. They'd swindled a famous gallery owner who was a bigger fraud than the replica they used as bait. The recollections ran up to the time they barely got away with their lives after a murderous trafficker discovered the gold brick of rhino horns they sold him were made of synthetic keratin. Henri taught Jack all of his tricks from how to stage a Thai gem to playing the fiddle game. But the most important lesson of all was the secret to every successful con—the mark had to be dishonest to begin with.

He blinked away the memories and fought off a shiver. The colorless room was purposely cold and the air was thick with disinfectant that did little to mask the scent of death. An occasional groan and whimper from a patient was about the only reminder he wasn't standing in a morgue.

Henri had been in wheelchair since his last stroke. He rarely left his houseboat. "So tell me, old friend," Jack whispered. "What lured you across the bay? Get a hankering for a bowl of cioppino at Tadich Grill or were you casing one last score? Lots of big money in the FiDi."

The only response was the rhythmic whoosh of the ventilator and the beep beep of the heart-monitoring machine. Jack left his friend's bedside and headed for the elevator.

Taylor S. glanced up. "I hope you know we're doing everything we can for him."

"Thanks. He deserves the best." He jotted down his phone number and gave it to her. "I'll drop by everyday but anything changes, call me. Day or night."

"Count on it."

"I wonder if you could do me a favor? There's another patient here I should check on. Can you see what room he's in? It would save me a trip down to Admitting."

"Well, aren't you the Good Samaritan. What's his name?"

"Fabro," Jack said. "Stefan Fabro."

"I could locate him by ward if you told me what he's in for."

"Sorry. All I got was a text from a friend who lives out of town asking me to see how he's doing. They're cousins."

"Cousins, huh?" Taylor S. gave a wry smile and then made a few strokes on the keyboard. "Here you go. Mr. Fabro is on the fourth floor. A private room." As she read some more, her eyebrows resembled a bow pulling taut. "Oh my. Your friend's cousin, handsome? The chart says he was shot. Twice."

2

Thunder boomed and whitecaps drummed hard on the ferry's hull. Sea lions hauled out on Alcatraz's rocky shore chimed in with their own roars. The pylons marking Sausalito's wharf were a moving target as the ferry heaved to. None of the passengers complained at the hard landing and a few even applauded when the deckhands made fast. Jack was the first one down the bucking gangplank. He broke into a jog when he hit Gate 5 Road and reached Henri's houseboat in record time. The brown shingle cottage with blue trimmed windows and matching flower boxes sat atop a converted gravel barge permanently moored in a slip at the end of the dock.

Jack whistled as he approached. "Hey Chagall. Here boy. Here boy."

Henri's white standard poodle was nowhere to be seen. Jack went aboard and peered through the houseboat's front windows. No Chagall. He tried the door but it was locked. He found the hide-a-key in a metal sea turtle with a removable shell. The cottage was cold inside and the air damp but at least it didn't smell of dead dog.

The interior reflected the houseboat's owner whose mantra was a place for everything and everything in its place. Framed plein air seascapes adorned the walls. They were Henri LeConte originals. He never sold his own work even though his evocative style and meticulous technique would've commanded high prices. Henri dreaded the thought of someone forging him. Jack thumbed through a pile of papers stacked on the chart table, a few bills, some receipts, and a couple of old racing forms. He didn't expect to find anything. Henri was too much of a pro to leave anything lying around that told a story he didn't want telling.

Jack turned to the galley. It was wide enough for Henri to navigate in his wheelchair. Jack checked the dish rack next to the sink. It held a single coffee cup and a silver dog bowl. Both were washed and dried. A single piece of paper was fastened to the door of the refrigerator by magnets. It was a schedule for the month. A name was typed in each square. Alison was Monday, Tuesday, and Thursday. Rainey was Wednesday and Friday. Ji-min was Saturday and Sunday. The same three names were printed at the bottom of the page with phone numbers next to them. They represented the latest semester at the College of Marin's nursing program. The houseboat was a revolving door for students picking up extra cash between classes. The only one Jack recalled meeting was Rainey. She was a blonde with red framed glasses that rode low on a pert nose. He raised his phone and snapped a picture of the schedule.

A door led to Henri's stateroom. The furnishings suggested an age gone by, a time when men wore double-breasted suits and carried monogrammed sterling silver cigarette cases, men who spoke with vague accents and were quick to offer a light to a woman and always stood when introduced. Jack went straight to the dresser. It was a heavy bombé chest with short curved legs and a green marble top. Henri had showed him the false bottom in the bottom drawer and told him if anything ever happened to get over there fast and remove the contents. Jack triggered the hidden latch and reached inside when the floorboards creaked.

"Turn around and keep your hands up or I'll run you through," barked a voice graveled by decades of cigarettes.

Jack faced a man who could've been David Crosby's doppelgänger. His stringy shoulder-length hair receded like the tide. It was white and wild, his horseshoe moustache the same. A flowered shirt couldn't contain his potbelly. What Jack concentrated on most was a rusty three-pronged spear attached to a long wooden handle.

"I'm warning you, don't get stupid. You may got some years on me but you're also the one at the business end of my puss sticker."

"Steady there, friend. Henri sent me. Name's Jack McCoul. You know he's in the hospital, right? SF General. A heart attack. I came over to check on Chagall. You seen him?"

"You won't find him in that drawer, now will you? Save your bullshit for the cops."

Jack sized him up. Being quirky and colorful was the unwritten rule for belonging to Sausalito's floating neighborhood and antiestablishmentarianism was as firmly entrenched as a joint for breakfast and tantric sex.

"Fine by me. We'll let them sort this out." Jack held up the front door key. "I have Henri's permission to be here. The cops will probably ask you too. You know how they are about trespassers. They also might get a bit skittish if you're wielding a weapon when they storm the castle."

The man made a spitting noise. "Screw the cops. I was at Berkeley in '64. Got a scar in the back of my head where a pig laid me out with a club to prove it. I was a roadie for the Stones at Altamont in '69. Cops broke my wrist slapping the cuffs on."

"Then maybe it'd be easier all the way around if we're both gone by the time they get here."

"Ah, no one's coming. You think I'd ask them for help? We watch out for our own here. Been a problem with break-ins lately. Punks looking to make a quick buck by snatching and grabbing. I catch 'em, I'll give 'em a taste of my puss sticker here." He jabbed the trident again.

"Puss sticker?"

"Octopus. They hole up along the breakwater. I can get at 'em in low tide. I sell 'em to the sushi joints. Hey, Social Security and Medicare only go so far."

"Have any idea where Chagall is?"

The man's moustache made an even taller arch. "Mutt's at the pound."

"How do you know that?"

"Because I took him, that's why." He lowered the trident. "Damn hound was howling in the rain. I live two houseboats down and the racket kept me and my old lady up all night. Hey, a man's got to get his z's on."

Jack breathed in, breathed out. It was a yoga technique Katie showed him to control emotions. Sometimes it worked. Usually it didn't. "He's an old dog. You didn't wonder why he was left outside?"

The strings of white hair swung like the frayed cuffs of a pair of '60s bell-bottoms. "Don't blame me. I couldn't take him to my place. My old lady, she's into cats. Got six."

"How long has he been at the pound?"

"Since yesterday. It's not like they're going to gas him right away. This is Marin County. Even rats are protected. I figured Henri could deal with it when he got back. I didn't know nothing about a heart attack." The man rubbed his oversized moustache. "Hey, you think there's a chance this boat slip, you know, if he doesn't make it, might come up for rent? It's the best one on the dock."

Jack blew out air. "Get out of here. Now. And I'm not asking."

"Okay, okay. But just so you know, I'm not a cat person. Really. You can ask my old lady."

After the man left, Jack removed a manila envelope from the hidey-hole in the bombé chest and took a set of car keys hanging from a hook near the front door. He locked it behind him.

THE DOWNPOUR LET up and the clouds started to break apart. Curtains of soft rain hung between shafts of light, the drops shimmering as if pieces of polished crystal dangled from heaven's chandelier. Jack watched from behind the wheel of Henri's burgundy Citroën as he steered across the Golden Gate Bridge. The bug-shaped classic had started right up, and he guessed the nurses took it for regular spins because Henri had stopped driving after his first stroke.

To the east a pair of tugboats escorted a tanker toward Anchorage Nine, a deepwater moorage a long homerun past the right field wall of the Giants' ballpark and within view from Jack's fourth-floor loft. Downtown glistened from a fresh washing of rain. Silhouettes of more than a dozen high-rise construction cranes etched the skyline, further testament to the tech boom's transformation of San Francisco into one of the mightiest powerhouses in the Pacific Rim. Jack was torn by the promise of so much wealth. On one hand, it meant more opportunity for him, on the other, it meant the loss of the soul of the city he loved. It also portended the burst of a bubble that was sure to come just as it had every time greed outpaced common sense. Tech shared that with a well-executed con.

Midday traffic heading into the city was light, and the

Citroën moved at a steady clip despite its age and dubious engineering. Chagall rode in the back seat, noshing on a bagel and cream cheese. It was his favorite treat and Jack had picked up a dozen before springing him from the Humane Society.

A manila envelope lay on the passenger seat. Jack had quickly checked it contents. It contained a sheaf of papers, a safety deposit key, and a blurry color photocopy of a snapshot of a woman holding the hand of a little girl who looked to be two or three. Their clothing gave no sense of time and the background held no clues to location.

Jack knew most of Henri's history but not all. He was a self-proclaimed ladies' man and said of the artists he forged—be it Vermeer, Gaugin, Matisse, or Picasso—that none ever came close to portraying the true essence of a woman. A real woman, he explained, exhibited more strength, beauty, complexity, and mystery in all its guises than all of the masterpieces combined. "The best men can do is accept the fact that what we see is only what they choose to share. The equivalent of the universe awaits discovery behind their eyes, their smiles, their hearts."

Henri confessed to having only one true love in his life. He'd told Jack the tragic story of Madhuri, a member of an Indian dance troupe he met on a luxury liner when he was working as the ship's artist-in-residence. The pair fell instantly in love, vowed to marry, and quit their shipboard jobs when they reached Mumbai so she could introduce him to her family. When they arrived they learned her brother owed a fortune in gambling losses to a local crime boss. Henri hatched a con to pay off his future brother-in-law's debts but the scheme went awry and Madhuri was taken hostage as collateral. He raced home to California to raise the money but before he could return and buy her freedom, Madhuri was said to have killed herself after being traded to a sex trafficker. Henri never forgave himself.

Jack passed through the tollbooth. Scanners had replaced humans but he wasn't concerned whether the Citroën had a FasTrak or not. He was too busy thinking about the photo. Despite the photocopy's blurriness, he could see the woman's hair was dark and so were her eyes. The little girl's hair was raven too but her skin was fair and her eyes blue. So were Henri's.

3

It was a five-minute walk from the parking garage to Abuelita's in the Mission District. Jack wore a Giants cap pulled down low and his collar turned up high. He still got wet. So did Chagall. The heavy rains were a welcome relief to drought-stricken California and a novelty to the army of tech workers who'd followed the money to San Francisco in recent years. By the time he pushed open the door to the Mexican restaurant, his shoes were soaked and his jeans plastered to his legs. The lunch crowd was larger than normal. The weather called for hearty fare, and bowls of *poblano albóndigas* and platters of *carnitas en salsa verde* were flying from the kitchen as fast as the seventy-year-old chef could fill them.

A big man with "Herald" tattooed on his neck in gothic letters and framed by angel wings was manning the bar. Hark didn't waste time with a bottle opener but popped the caps off beers by striking them on the edge of the metal sink. He grinned at Jack and motioned him toward an empty stool.

"What, you qualify for a service dog now? A shot of tequila warm you right up. Two'll dry you from the inside out. Your *perro* want one too?"

Jack shrugged out of his jacket. He accepted a bar towel and mopped his face. "It's been so long I'd forgotten rain's wet. No complaints though. Let it pour. Everyone's tired of rationing." He put a bowl of tortilla chips on the floor. The poodle dug right in.

"This El Niño is *muy macho*," Hark said. "Good for business too."

Jack hooked a thumb at the overflowing restaurant. "Nice of you to help your grandma out during the noon rush."

"It's good for my business too. People forgot how to drive in the rain. We're getting all sorts of fender benders in addition to our usual clientele." Hark had opened a custom paint and body shop around the corner after completing two tours in Afghanistan. Enlisting was the option he chose rather than taking a jolt at Stockton Correctional during his days as a gang-banger. His '64 Chevy Impala lowrider was a rolling advertisement.

Jack toasted him. "To slick streets and the return of long, hot showers."

Hark poured himself a shot. "Amen to that. So what's with the dog?"

"You don't recognize him? It's Chagall. Henri LeConte's poodle."

Hark leaned over the counter. "He's bigger than I remember. Plus he needs a haircut. What, things so tough you got to take up dog walking now?"

"Henri had a heart attack. He's in the ICU at SF General."

"*Chingame*," the big man cursed softly. "He going make it?"

"Hope so. I only found out this morning. Wonder Boy told me. Don't ask me how he knew but that's Wonder for you. I went straight to the hospital and then over to Sausalito to pick up Chagall. You know how Henri is about him."

A server brought a bowl of soup without Jack having to ask for it. He glanced at the kitchen. Hark's grandmother stood in the doorway. She waved a ladle at him and flashed a gold-tooth smile. The restaurant had been Jack's second home when he was growing up. It offered a refuge from the fists and empty bottles of Guinness that flew whenever his old man returned from fighting a fire and tried to douse the flames that raged within him.

"Must be serious, they bring Henri all the way over here."

Jack spooned some soup and chased it with tequila. "That's just it. Henri wasn't home when he went down. He was here in the city."

Hark studied an order ticket before opening a couple of Pacificos and a Mexican fruit-flavored soft drink. He placed the bottles on a tray. "One of his private nurses with him? I forget their names they change so often."

"Alison, Ji-min, and Rainey. That's the newest trio. The EMT report didn't mention it and I got the impression he was alone."

"What do you think he was up to?"

"Don't know but I'm going to look into it. I owe it to him in case it's something rather than nothing."

"You need help, you don't got to ask. I always respected him."

"I'll let you know."

"How's Katie taking it? She's sweet on the old man."

"I haven't told her yet. She'd already left for work when Wonder called me. I don't want to tell her over the phone. I'll wait until tonight."

"She still running flat out?"

"Yeah. Opened another gym."

"That makes, what, three, four in the last few months?"

"Four. The newest is in the East Bay."

"Same as the others, in a 'hood where even Starbucks won't go? It's like she's on a crusade or something, all due respect. Bringing health and fitness to the people by teaching yoga and yogurt in the land of Big Macs."

Jack let it go. He didn't want to get into it about why he thought his wife was taking her enterprise to a whole new level ever since her pregnancy was confirmed. He'd learned the hard way after he suggested she should dial back on her workload. Katie spent the next hour setting him straight about women's bodies being their own, birthing rituals from the Inuits to Saharan nomads, glass ceilings, Frida Kahlo, Barbie dolls, and men having invented war, porn, and polygamy. There'd been some frost in the air ever since, so he doubled down on watching what he said and trying to get used to the idea that his world was about to get rocked harder than any earthquake he'd ever experienced.

Hark refilled their glasses. The tequila was the color of straw and the smell conjured images of blue agave stalks curing over a bed of mesquite coals.

Jack chased a spicy meatball around the bowl. "Guess who I ran into at the hospital? When I was waiting to see Henri." He chewed the meatball. "Grace Millefiori."

"*Chingame.* Don't tell me you talked to her? Ah, you did. I can see her reflection still burning in your eyes. She still casts a spell, that *bruja.* Didn't you learn nothing?"

"I learned plenty from Grace all right."

Jack and Grace met on a job, a complicated big store using a cast of players targeting a mark who traded commodities as a laundry service for fat cats looking to dodge taxes. The mutual attraction was incendiary from the start, but just as wildfires and lightning burn hot and bright and fast, everything in their path got scorched—friends, enemies, relatives, themselves. After Prague when time and distance helped cool the flames, Jack told himself they were too much alike. If they'd stayed together, the absence of checks and balances would have left them dancing on the edge of a razor blade until one slipped and either took the other one down with them or forced a choice between risking a grab or letting them fall.

"She's been off the radar screen for a long time now," Hark said. "What's she doing back? More to the point, how did she know you'd be at the hospital?"

"I was too early for visiting hours and she happened to spot me on her way to see her husband. He's a patient there."

"SF General, what, it covers four square blocks? You're sitting in some out-of-the-way corner thumbing through a three-year-old *Reader's Digest* and Grace Millefiori happens to pass by on her way to see her sick hubby?"

"Something like that."

"Aren't you the dude always saying coincidences are for scientists?"

"Scientologists. Coincidences are for... Never mind. But it's the way it went down. She was as surprised as me. We only spoke for a minute."

"Uh-huh." Hark filled another drink order and topped off their tequilas while he was at it. "This husband. This husband of Grace Millefiori-who-broke-a-thousand-hearts-including-yours. She say why he was in the hospital?"

"No but I found out later."

"Don't tell me you visited him?"

"A nurse told me."

"Because you sweet-talked her into it."

"I admit I was curious."

When Hark rolled his eyes, the scar from a tattooed tear he had removed by laser bounced. "You ain't learned anything." The big man wrung a bar towel. His biceps stretched the sleeves of his untucked flannel shirt. "Okay. I'll bite. What's wrong with him, the husband?"

"A case of lead poisoning. Seems he got in the way of a couple of rounds."

"Fuck me." Hark downed his tequila and slammed the empty glass on the bar. "And you say it's all a coincidence? Hell, *ese*, knowing Grace, she the one probably shot him to set up whatever it is she's setting you up for."

Jack grinned. Whenever his friend swore in English, he knew he really meant it.

4

The loft's windows were wide open and the groans of ships straining against their anchors couldn't drown out Chagall's snores. Jack sat at the dining room table with the dog curled at his feet and watched the reflection of the Bay Bridge lights waver on the inky waters. His hand and ear burned as if the phone carried a live electrical current.

"How did you get this number?" he said again.

"Come on, Jack. Give me some credit." Grace Millefiori's laugh was light but couldn't hide an undercurrent.

"What do you want?"

"Is this really the way you want to play it?"

"Which way?"

"Indifferent. We both know that's a stalling tactic." She breathed into the phone. He could all but feel the wingbeats. "I've been thinking about you. Seeing you, well, it brought back a lot of memories. A lot of feelings."

"So does a twenty-hour interrogation by the Czech *policie*. Do you know they actually do use rubber hoses?"

"That's not funny."

"What do you want?"

"Help. I don't have anyone else to turn to."

"If it's about money, try Jimmie Fang. He only charges twenty points vig a day. Your husband need a ride home from the hospital? I hear Uber has ambulances now. They won't even tag on a cleanup fee if the passenger leaves blood stains from a couple of gunshots."

"That's my Jack. I knew you still cared enough to check."

"That's my Grace," he parried back. "The men in your life always wind up like Swiss cheese."

"What happened to Stefan is not what you think."

"I don't think anything. You need help, you dialed the wrong number."

He wondered if she hung up but his phone didn't signal a disconnect. She finally spoke. "I saw Henri this afternoon. It doesn't look good for him, does it? It's so incredibly sad. I feel as if one of the last true gentlemen is about to leave us and the world will be the poorer for it. He was like a father to me. I've always loved him."

Jack swallowed his surprise. Of course Grace would recall how much he hated hospitals. Of course she'd wonder why he was there. He was slipping since getting out of the game. There was no denying it.

"Leave Henri out of this, okay?"

Grace didn't say anything. She just breathed.

Jack sighed. "Okay, what do you want? I'm not saying I'll help but maybe I can steer you to someone who can."

Nobody said thank you like Grace. She put everything a person wanted to hear into it, make them believe they were capable of walking barefoot across red-hot lava for her, and hear a promise of gratitude that would take them to a place beyond their wildest fantasies. Jack had seen it work on plenty of marks before. Cold-blooded criminals, steely-nerved tycoons, and larcenous financiers all fell under the spell of those two little words. So had he.

Her exhale echoed across the phone and carried with it a memory of the moans she made when making love. "It's about water. Our water. Our vineyard's. They're trying to steal it and they'll stop at nothing until they get it. They already tried to kill Stefan."

"It's called 911. You push the numbers on your phone. When they answer you shout, 'Help. Send the police.' Sometimes you have to shout it twice."

"I did but it's the sheriff's department out here and they acted like they couldn't care less."

Jack's eyes swept across the bay. The lights of Oakland wore halos in the mist. Tires swished on the streets below. "Okay, I'll bite. Who's trying to steal your water and why?"

"His name is Jonathan Gossamer. He wants you to believe he's the Zuckerberg of hedge funds. Farmers control most of the water in the valley and he's going after their rights. It's all very complicated and better explained in person. Could you come to my place? Please?"

"Don't people know it's been raining for a solid month? Okay, here's what you do. Tell him to look up at the sky and open his mouth. Turkeys do it all the time and when they do, they drown. Problem solved."

"This isn't a laughing matter. The storms won't change history. Water is gold but even more, it's power. Jonathan Gossamer knows that." She took another deep breath and added a quaver when she let it go. "I need you, Jack. I really do. I know I hurt you but if you knew why I left you, you'd understand. You used to care about me. If nothing else, please help for what we once had. Please?"

Before Jack could say anything the loft's front door banged

open. "Henri? Is Henri here? What's his car doing in the garage?"

Chagall scrambled from beneath the table. The dog's stump of a tail was louder than a metronome as he beelined toward Katie.

"I got to go," Jack said.

"Is that your wife? She must be something special to get you to settle down. I'd love to meet her."

Jack's face tightened. "You got my number. Text me your coordinates. No promises though." And he swiped off before Grace could say another word.

Katie scratched the long-legged poodle behind his ears but she trained her eyes on Jack. "What's Chagall doing here? Where's Henri?"

Jack placed his palms on her shoulders. "Henri had a heart attack, babe. A big one."

She gasped. "Is he..."

"No, he's in the ICU."

"Then what are we doing here? We need to get over there right away."

"He's in a coma."

"That doesn't mean a thing. There's plenty of medical evidence proving the benefits of visitors. Brain wave monitors show increased activity among comatose patients whenever their loved ones are at their bedside."

Katie had graduated from Berkeley magna cum laude and was headed to med school when she carved a different path based on her own theory of alternative healing methods featuring regular exercise, healthy eating, and fashionable attire. "Feel great, be great" was her company's slogan.

"I'm sure you're right but we have to wait. Visiting hours are done for the night. I'll drive you over first thing in the morning."

"When did it happen?"

"A couple of days ago. I got the news this morning."

"And you didn't think to call me?"

"It was the first thing I did think of but..."

"But what?"

A dozen answers ran through his mind but he heard how they sounded. "I didn't want to tell you on the phone because... Ah, hell, babe, after I saw him lying there, I suppose I didn't want to hear myself say it out loud."

They stood without saying another word but plenty was being said between them. Katie's expression started to soften and with it so did some of the tension that had been festering since the day she'd told him she was pregnant and his immediate reaction hadn't exactly involved a backflip and cheer.

"So you rushed right over to Sausalito to rescue Chagall."

"Well, yeah, he's an old dog. It was pouring. You know how Henri spoils him."

Katie threw her arms around him. "You are so sweet."

Jack tried to reply but couldn't get the words out because her lips were locked on his.

THE RAIN PICKED up again and a stiff wind came with it. The pelting against the windows woke Jack. He slid out of bed to check all were shut.

"Don't step on Chagall," Katie murmured from somewhere beneath the comforter.

The warning came in the nick of time. The dog was asleep in a nest of blankets at the foot of the bed.

"Where are you going?"

"Battening down the hatches," Jack said.

"I thought that's what you've been doing all night, sailor."

Jack laughed. Hearing her use the language that was all their own—a language where teasing was a symbol of trust, where all the *i*'s didn't need dotting or the *t*'s crossed—triggered a release more powerful than when they'd been making love. He hopped over the poodle and slid his hands under the comforter.

"You know we skipped dinner. How about I make a midnight snack? We can eat right here. Cheese omelet and a protein shake sound good?"

"You're going to drink a whey and kale smoothie?"

"Uh, sure. Why not?"

Now it was Katie's turn to laugh. "There's a split of Schramsberg in the fridge. At least I can enjoy a little bubbly vicariously."

"I'll be right back."

"Don't forget to bring Chagall something."

Jack pulled on sweats and made his way to the kitchen while letting sleeping dogs lay. In the light of the open refrigerator door, he whipped up six eggs and folded in shredded cheese and added pinches of sea salt, sage, and thyme. As the omelet bubbled he checked his phone. A text from a number with a 209 area code contained a link. He clicked it and a map and directions to Clemens filled the screen. He didn't know much about the town outside of the fact it was named for a favorite author. One of Mark Twain's famous quips immediately sprang to mind: "Whisky is for drinking and water is for fighting over."

When the eggs were finished, he halved the omelet, slid the portions onto plates, and ferried everything back to bed.

Katie was sitting up. The bedside lamp bathed her breasts in a golden glow. Jack tossed a plain bagel next to Chagall and placed the tray down. He was no sooner beneath the comforter when the sounds of canine munching reached his ears.

Katie was no less ravenous. She was halfway through wolfing down her eggs by the time Jack poured his champagne. "Do you know how many calories get burned during sex?" she said between forkfuls.

"I suppose that depends on a number of factors."

"It's one of the best workouts ever. Cardio, aerobic, core. You use all of your muscles."

"I can think of at least one."

She punched his shoulder. They finished the omelet in a satisfying silence. Jack was washing down the last bite when Katie said, "Who were you talking to when I got home? You sounded tense."

Jack kept the swallow of champagne down. "Somebody from the past looking for advice. How was your day?"

Katie tapped the corner of her eye. "When you say 'somebody' you mean a woman. Who is she?"

Jack gave up questioning Katie's intuition long ago. He'd relied on it to get out of jams more than once.

"We used to work together." He felt her gaze. "Truth is we were more than that. It was before I met you." He polished off the rest of his champagne and filled another glass. "Long, long before."

"Oh, she's the *other* woman. I always wondered who she was. What's her name?"

"Come on. The past is past. How's that protein shake taste?"

"Do you know why the Quechua Indians believe the future is behind you and the past in front of you?"

"I don't but I have a feeling I'm about to find out."

"It's because you can see the past but not the future."

"I *see* your point."

"Ha, ha. You know what Buddha teaches? The past, present, and future are all connected. *'Das-pa, da-tla-ba*, and *ma-'ong-ba*."

Jack waved his glass in surrender. "You win. Her name is Grace Millefiori."

"That's very pretty. A thousand flowers. Italian, huh? What does she look like?"

"Really?"

"I don't know why you're so worried about telling me. Of course, there was another woman in your life. Just as there was another man in mine. The fact that we had those but chose each other makes what we have even stronger."

Jack couldn't forget the other man. That's because it was Terrence Dolan, a detective with SFPD's Robbery and Homicide Division. Terry and Jack had been classmates at St. Joseph's before either knew Katie. One was an altar boy, the other a boy who used the altar to run three-card monte games on. Terry met Katie first and asked her to marry him. She went to Nepal to think his proposal over. By chance she met Jack in a Kathmandu teahouse. She called it destiny; Jack called it damn good luck. Terry never got over being thrown over, and the fact that it was for his longtime adversary made his loss even more humiliating. He made it his life's ambition to put Jack behind bars once and for all.

"So tell me what Grace looks like?"

Jack told her but left out the tattoo.

"What does she want?"

"She and her husband have a winery in the Central Valley. There's some kind of dispute over water. I don't know what she thinks I can do about it."

"So she's married. That's good. Can't her husband deal with it?"

"He met a couple of obstacles."

"Then of course you have to help. It's your duty." Chagall got up and padded over to Katie's side of the bed. She began scratching his ears.

"Trust me, I don't owe Grace a thing. She's hardly the damsel-in-distress type."

"That's not what I meant. You have a duty to close the circle with her given your past together, your *'das-pa*. Your *da-tla-ba* can't proceed to *ma-'ong-ba* if your *'das-pa* is still out of sorts."

"Sounds worse than dengue fever."

"I'm serious. It's not only your *ma-'ong-ba* at risk, it's ours too." She cradled her stomach. "You'd better go see her first thing in the morning."

"But what about Henri?"

"I'll take Chagall with me. There's plenty of medical literature about the healing properties of pets."

"Have it your way, but don't blame me if my *'das* jumps up and bites me in the ass."

5

Eastbound traffic on the Bay Bridge was traveling at the limit. Bright white cables strung from a mast-like tower held the twin skyways aloft. The new eastern span came with a hefty price tag and an even heftier promise. Its backers swore it would withstand any earthquake imaginable. While Jack appreciated the sleek design and sailboat-like profile, experience taught him to be wary of hype and guarantees. It wouldn't be the first time taxpayers bought a George C. Parker, a con named for a smooth-talking fleecer who made his bones in the early 1900s selling the Brooklyn Bridge over and over again.

Jack stuck to the far right lane as he dialed and drove. His calls to the first two student nurses listed on Henri's refrigerator went straight to voicemail. His third try was picked up on the second ring.

"Is this Rainey?" he asked.

"It is. Who's calling, please?"

Jack told her. "We met at Henri LeConte's. I'm an old friend."

"Dark hair and Irish, right? Brooding brows but laughing eyes. Yes, I remember you but not the *old* part. How are you?"

"I'm calling about Henri. Did you know he's in the hospital?"

"Oh, no. What happened?"

"He had a heart attack."

"Oh, my god. How is he?"

"In pretty rough shape actually."

"I just saw him last Friday. When did it happen?

"Monday."

"I'm surprised Alison didn't tell me. She does Mondays."

"It's unclear if she was with him. I tried calling her but only got voicemail."

"I'm sure she'll call you back. Always respond is one of the first things they teach us at nursing school."

"You know her well?"

"Pretty well. I mean, the program's small so we share some classes. We occasionally overlap doing rounds at Marin General. Did you speak to Ji-min? She's Henri's weekend nurse."

"I couldn't reach her either." He slowed for a car switching into his lane. "What's she like?"

"Quiet but I haven't had much time to get to know her. Ji-min is new. A reentry."

"You know what she did before coming to nursing school?"

"Not really. Tech probably. That's what everybody does until they find out how soulless it is. Most of the companies treat their workers like they're disposable. They call layoffs 'graduations.' Ugh."

Jack pictured Rainey making a face, the big red framed glasses sliding down her pert nose. "Wednesdays are your days. Didn't you wonder where Henri was?"

"I didn't work that day. I had a makeup exam for my boards. It took hours. Ugh. I told the school's job center I had a conflict and needed a sub. I also sent texts to Alison and Ji-min to let them know so they'd have first shot at it. Everybody's always looking for extra hours. It's so expensive living here."

"Did either respond?"

"Now that you mention it, I don't think they did. Oh well, everybody's super busy."

Jack reached land. Palm trees rustled in the center divider. Three freeway choices lay ahead. He took the middle course toward Interstate 580.

"How did Henri seem on Friday?"

"Good. I mean there were no signs of an impending MI or anything like it. In fact, he seemed better than ever. Excited and full of energy. He wanted to go out to lunch and run some errands."

"You take his car?"

"Uh-huh. He likes to keep the battery charged. It's French, like him. A classic. Like him too." Rainey laughed and then caught herself. "God, I hope he's going to be okay."

"Where did you go?"

"Sam's Anchor Café for lunch. It's his favorite."

Jack knew the Tiburon haunt. It was one of Henri's regular hangouts.

"And the errands?"

"Let's see, we went to the Whole Foods over in Mill Valley and the pharmacy. Oh, and FedEx too."

"Henri ship something?"

"He wanted to make some copies."

"Of what?"

"Photos. You don't see them like that anymore."

"Like what?"

"Prints somebody sends you by snail mail. Nobody does that, not even my grandmother. She's obsessed with Facebook."

"You mean they came in an envelope. Did it have a return address?"

"I suppose so but I didn't really look. Why?"

"I'm just trying to figure out if there's anyone else that needs to be contacted," he said quickly. "Let them know what happened to Henri."

"That's a good idea. I don't know if it's any help but the envelope was purple and the handwriting looked feminine. You know, cursive with loops."

"Did you get a glimpse of the photos?"

"Just the top one. It was a mother and child."

"Did Henri tell you who they were?"

"No and I didn't have time to ask. My phone rang. It was the job center. They wanted to know if I could do some extra hours. I stepped outside to talk. When I hung up Henri was all done copying. He paid for it himself and wheeled his chair back to the car. I took him home. I had to leave a little early. You know, because of the phone call. Another girl got sick and they needed me to fill in. It happens all the time."

"Did you see what he did with the originals and the envelope they came in?"

"No. I had to put the groceries away, check to make sure his meds were all in order, and then run. He said he was fine. And he was. I wouldn't've left him if he wasn't. Look, thanks for telling me about Henri but I have to go. I'm late for class. If I think of anything else, I'll give you a call, okay?"

"Sure, one last thing. Do you know where Alison and Ji-min live?"

"Alison has an apartment in the city. In the Richmond on Clement Street. I'm not sure about Ji-min. I want to say the Marina but I'm not positive. She keeps to herself."

Jack said thanks and clicked off.

He steered the Citroën through the MacArthur Maze. It was bogged down as usual. I-580 was the most direct route but a wall of red taillights up ahead forced him onto Highway 24 instead. Three interchanges later he was tooling down a two-lane blacktop built on dikes along the Sacramento-San Joaquin

Rivers Delta, the state's plumbing system. The route meant more miles but he didn't mind. It gave him extra time to steel himself for what he knew would be anything but a simple reunion between old friends.

CLEMENS WAS a blink-and-miss-it town surrounded by a patchwork quilt of dairy farms, orchards, and vineyards. A two-lane highway served as Main Street. The storefronts lining it couldn't agree on a uniform architectural style. A Spanish stucco housing The Jumping Frog Café stood shoulder to shoulder with a wooden saloon with a false front complete with swinging doors and gold rush-era lettering on the windows. The barber pole out front of the redbrick shop next door appeared to have stopped spinning when mullets went out of style. A barnlike structure advertised "20% off on all antiques, new and used." City Hall and the Sheriff's Department shared a cinderblock building painted the color of dust.

Jack slowed at the only traffic signal. It was stuck on yellow. He checked both directions. The road to his left disappeared into a grove of almond trees. To the right ran a drab row of modest look-alike single-story houses and beyond them vineyards. According to his map app, the turnoff to Grace's was in a mile.

He crossed a bridge spanning a concrete aqueduct. The Central Valley was veined with them. The longest transported water from the Delta to Los Angeles. Jack slowed going over so he could take a look. The canal was nearly full and no fences protected it. *So much for safeguarding liquid gold*, he thought.

A robotic voice on his phone told him to turn right up ahead. He was about to hit the turn signal when the rearview mirror flashed red and blue. The whoop-whoop of a siren followed. Jack checked the speedometer. He wasn't even doing thirty.

"A Georgia speed trap," he muttered and pulled to the side.

The patrol car was white and green. The light bar on the roof sported antenna quills. Jack eyed the mirror as he waited for the cop to get out of the car. A few minutes passed so he rolled down his window and then placed his hands at ten and two on the steering wheel. The cop finally approached. She wore a Smokey Bear hat and looked in her mid-thirties. A gold star shined above the left breast pocket of her khaki uniform. A name tag was pinned above the right pocket. Deputy Santos.

"License and registration, please."

"Sure but you should know my license is in my wallet and I'm sitting on it. The registration is in the glove box. Along with another thing you'll want to see. Okay if I reach for them?"

"What's the other thing?" Her tone was suspicious.

"When you ran the license plate you learned the car is registered to a Henri LeConte of Sausalito. You would've also found out he's in his seventies. Since I'm obviously not of that age, I'm obviously not Henri LeConte. I don't want anyone to get the wrong idea here." He shot a look her. "I got a legal document proves I'm his conservator. That makes me entitled to use his assets while managing his affairs, including his car."

"Hand them over, please."

Jack extracted the license first. Then he popped open the glove box and pulled out the registration and a durable power of attorney he'd ginned up that morning. Boy Scouts hadn't cornered the market on always being prepared.

The deputy read the documents. "Your license says you're from San Francisco. Are you always in the habit of traveling with letters from your lawyer?"

"I'd answer you but I'd have to call him first to see if it's okay," he said with a smile but she didn't return it. "So why did you pull me over? I wasn't speeding."

"The other way around." Her voice was firm but neutral. "We get people who stop on the bridge and throw junk in the canal. Beer cans, old tires, even refrigerators. It's a real hassle to fish out."

"But I didn't throw anything in nor would I. If you want, I can put someone on the phone who can vouch for that."

"Let me guess, your lawyer."

"No, my wife. She'll tell you I'm pretty housebroken by now. I don't even leave my socks on the floor anymore."

That earned a slight crinkle at the corner of her eyes.

"I'll make sure not to sightsee on the bridge next time I pass through. Can I have my license back?"

She held the documents aloft. "One more thing. Just so *you* don't get the wrong idea. This is a very neighborly community. Most of the families have lived here for generations. They work hard and treat each other with respect. But that's not to say law enforcement doesn't have a role. Rural areas have their share of issues too."

"Like a winemaker getting shot in the chest?"

Her wide brim hat didn't budge. "What do you know about that?"

"Only what his wife told me. We're old friends."

Deputy Santos eyes narrowed. If she wore mascara it didn't show. "And what is it that you do, Mr. McCoul?"

"Like the POA there says. I help people out."

She handed him back the paperwork. "Drive safe. You'll find the roads here aren't like they are in the big city. Few things are."

6

Several hens scratched in the front yard. Two were brown and ordinary looking, and the others were feathered kaleidoscopes. A modern farmhouse designed to look old stood on a rise. It was white clapboard with a covered veranda built to provide plenty of shade. Summer in the valley stayed in the hundreds for days at a time and the nights were only a bit cooler but it was hard to imagine that kind of weather now. The sky was filled with clouds that resembled a herd of Black Angus ready to stampede. A fecund odor rose from the earth. Robins stalked worms in a garden abandoned until spring. Row upon row of vines naked of leaves stretched in every direction.

Jack checked his phone when he got out of the car. Neither of the student nurses had returned his call but there was a text from Katie with a couple of photos attached. One showed Chagall staring at Henri's bed through the glass partition in the ICU. The other was a selfie with Taylor S. "I asked her to be our midwife," Katie messaged. "She rocks."

"Over here." The sound of Grace's voice turned him away from the phone.

She was standing in front of a building with no windows; the walls were made of poured concrete and painted to look like limestone except for one patch that was scarred by fire. Grace's jeans were tucked into knee-high rubber boots. She wore a brown canvas jacket and a man's felt hat. Her cheeks were flushed from excitement, exertion or both.

"Come on and I'll show you where all the magic happens. I'm just finishing up." When Jack drew close she leaned in, kissed him lightly on the cheek, and then looped her arm through his. "I'm glad you came."

A large wooden sliding door was open wide enough for them to squeeze through. The air inside the winery was chilly and their breath hung like thought bubbles in a comic strip. Shiny stainless steel tanks stood floor to ceiling on both sides.

"They're fermenters," Grace explained as she checked gauges and fiddled with knobs. "Each holds 600 gallons. Do you know much about winemaking?"

"Only that I like my reds big and my whites dry."

"There's lots of chemistry involved. Stefan taught me. Wine-making is in his blood."

He followed her down the row of metal tanks and watched her work. "Where did you two meet?"

"Argentina. I was staying at a guesthouse on an *estancia* in Mendoza. That's a western province in the heart of winemaking country. It's big sky country. Lots of sunny valleys with the Andes as a backdrop. Postcard gorgeous. Stefan was a neighbor. He'd moved there a few years before."

They reached the end of the building. A large, wooden table was covered with bottles. Some were empty, others full. Some had plain white labels with notes handwritten on them, others were blank. Grace picked up a bottle, uncorked it, and sniffed.

She filled two glasses and handed him one. "Try this."

Jack drank without smelling the wine first. He didn't roll it in his mouth, make a woodchuck face and gargle, or spit it into a metal cuspidor either. The wine was full and round and very good.

"How come he left California?"

"Stefan wanted to get away from his family, the whole dynasty thing." Grace swirled her wine glass before taking a sip. "I started going on trips with him. He was visiting wineries throughout Argentina and Chile with the idea of starting an import/export business. I discovered a new world. Growing grapes. Making wine. Selling it. It turns out it's what I've been searching for my whole life. Must be my Italian heritage."

She gazed at him over her glass. The hat looked good on her. Real good. "You understand that's not a criticism of what you and I had. That was a different time in my life. A different world. I was different."

Jack noticed she didn't bat a lash when she said it. Grace had always been restless when they were together, always searching for the next big thing, and eager to adopt a new role in the cons they played. At times, especially after a score, it was as if she was uncomfortable being back in her own skin.

"You certainly learned how to make vino," he said. "This is a ninety pointer easy. A Sangiovese, right? Doing Italian varietals your idea?"

"As a matter of fact it is." She picked up the bottle by the neck. "Come on, time for lunch."

He followed her outside and across the yard. The Sierra Nevada formed the eastern horizon where storm clouds snagged on snowcapped peaks. Thunder rolled in the distance. A light rain began to fall in the valley.

The house was decorated in blond wood, white walls, and beige and taupe fabrics. Grace pulled off her boots and hung her hat and barn jacket on a brass hook. She wore a V-neck T-shirt with capped sleeves and walked barefoot. When they reached the kitchen, she flipped a wall switch that ignited flames in a gas fireplace. All the appliances were stainless steel. The range had six burners, two ovens, and a griddle. The sink was big enough to bathe in.

"Make yourself comfortable." Grace pointed to a stool at a granite-top island a little smaller than Guam. "I have a pot of minestrone I can heat up. There's bruschetta to go with it. That sound good? And antipasto, of course."

"Funny, I don't remember you being able to boil water. Need any help?"

"Not with cooking. Stopping Jonathan Gossamer, yes."

"You're sure he shot your husband?"

She filled two fresh glasses. "I doubt he pulled the trigger but I'm positive he gave the order. It was probably his body-guard. He never goes anywhere without him."

"What's this bodyguard like?"

"You know the type. It's as if he has no facial nerves." She moved her hand to mime a curtain going up and down.

"He have a name too?"

"I never heard it." Grace pulled things from the refrigerator: a soup pot with a lid on it, jars of olives and marinated artichoke hearts, a slab of prosciutto. "We were having dinner when a car came up the drive. We weren't expecting anyone but it's not all that unusual. People take a wrong turn."

She went to work slicing the Italian ham with a shiny thin knife. "A few minutes later there was a glow out the window. We went to take a look. A pickup truck—one of those kinds with enormous wheels and the suspension showing—was backing down the driveway but not before the driver threw a Molotov cocktail at our cellar. I wanted to turn the hose on the flames but

Stefan told me the water would only spread them. You could smell the gasoline. He grabbed an extinguisher we keep in the tool shed. While he was putting it out, I came back inside to call the sheriff. That's when he was shot."

"The fire was a setup. You get a look at the shooter?"

Grace's hair did the silent wave in the night treatment. "He was hiding in the vineyard. He used a rifle. A .22 caliber."

"That's what kids use for popping squirrels and crows."

She carved the air with the prosciutto knife. "It's also what really good pros use for hits. You know that."

Jack didn't contradict her. Guns had always been a sticking point between them. He believed if you needed a piece to work a con, the play was designed wrong from the get-go. Grace thought otherwise. Their last argument was over the Lady Hawk 9mm she'd hidden in her checked luggage on the flight to Prague. Jack told her it could've gotten them busted. She countered that a woman in their game always needed to have an edge. He wondered if she still had it.

"Sounds like your husband's lucky to be alive."

"He is. Especially since the shooter used hollow points. That shows the kind of person Jonathan Gossamer employs. He purposely picked the kind of ammo that bounces around to cause the most damage. One slug punctured Stefan's lung and he developed sepsis. We had to medevac him to San Francisco General's Trauma Center."

"When was that?"

"He's been there three days now."

"I mean when did he get shot."

"A week ago but things had been building up for a while."

"How many times have you met Gossamer?"

She went back to work preparing the meal and kept her eyes down. "He came here twice but Stefan talked to him on the phone a few times. It started with a cold call. He'd done some research about the Fabros and this vineyard and made it sound like he was Stefan's best friend. Everything started as polite and how he was here to help. Stefan turned him down flat. The next thing we know he's knocking on our front door. Again, all nice and friendly."

"And the other guy, the muscle?"

"He stayed by the car. At first I thought he was a driver but then I got a look at him up close. You could see it in his eyes: people are either enemies or collateral damage. He doesn't care which. Remember, we worked with a man like that once. It was a job we did in Europe. I forget his name. Russian, maybe. Georgian? Anyway, he had that same look."

"I take it your husband shut the door on Gossamer."

"He did. Stefan made some calls and learned that he'd approached a couple of other growers in the county trying to buy their rights too. Ready to eat?"

AFTER LUNCH they moved to the living room. It had an open beam ceiling and no TV. The couch was positioned in front of a floor-to-ceiling window that provided a view of grapevines planted in rows as straight as lasers. Grace took a seat crosswise and tucked her bare feet under an alpaca throw. Jack sat down on the couch too. He sipped from an espresso cup and watched clouds veined with lightning gather.

"You haven't told me why you moved back to California."

"Stefan and I wanted to make our own wine. Who knows, maybe even win an award or two. We tried to find property in Mendoza but land prices skyrocketed when the big international houses discovered Malbec grapes could be grown cheaper there than in France. Malbec is one of six grapes allowed to blend Bordeaux."

Jack acknowledged her expertise with a raised brow.

"We searched for property in Chile too but the government there, well, it's difficult for foreigners to buy land. Then clear out of the blue Stefan's mother called. Her health was declining and she wanted to mend fences. His father has been dead for some time."

Grace took a breath and waved her hand. "The farm here has been in the Fabro family for, well, forever. It's an entire section. That's 640 acres but not all of it is cultivated. At one time or another Stefan's great-grandfather owned half the county."

"So this is Stefan's inheritance," Jack said.

"Yes. When Stefan's mother called, he agreed to fly up. Her estate was a mess. A financial advisor had taken advantage of her after Stefan's father died. Stefan helped set things straight. He inventoried her holdings and discovered this section. It had all but been forgotten. He came over to look and found that many of the legacy vines were still alive. When people think of California wine they usually think of Napa and Sonoma but half the state's production is right here in the Central Valley. Long story short, we left Argentina, settled here, and went to work turning things around. This house? We were living in a migrant worker's shack until a few months ago. It's brand new."

"His mom still alive?"

"She lives in San Francisco. She's the silver-haired queen of the symphony and museum society set."

"The grapevines look manicured, almost industrial. Not what you usually picture. You know, gnarled trunks. Methuselahs."

"They're the secret to our success. Most of the production here was originally for table grapes and bulk wine. Chug-a-jug as you so poetically put it. But Stefan's a wiz when it comes to viticulture. He devised ways we could augment the soil to produce wine quality grapes from common stock. We've divided the section into different vineyards according to soil types. One has as much schist in the ground as Tuscany. The dirt is called *galestro*."

"You created your own slice of Italy right here? I'm impressed. Any chance you're making a Brunello with your Sangiovese grapes?"

She gave a knowing smile. "You've always liked Brunello. I'll bet that's what you and your wife drink on special occasions. Just like we used to."

His shrug was noncommittal.

Grace stretched her legs. The alpaca throw slipped off as she pressed her toes against his thigh. The nails were red. "I'm right about the Brunello, aren't I? Tell me about her. Do you have children?"

Jack wasn't about to hand Grace that kind of leverage. When she was on the grift, she was the slickest pickpocket of personal information he'd ever come across, a master when it came to using the three *s*'s to bait and turn a mark: surprise, secrets, and sex.

"What other kinds of soil are you making out here?" he asked.

"Okay, have it your way. Let's see, in another vineyard we leached out the carbonates in the soil, sped up oxidization, and created *terra rossa*. That's for our Cab. The grapes are still young. It's a work in progress."

"And all this takes water. A lot of water."

"You got it. Winemaking is water intensive to begin with but when you add all the soil augmentation we're doing, well, luckily we have plenty to go around."

"You mean rights to water."

"I should've known you'd do your homework. *A* plus."

"From what I understand there are old rights and then there are new rights. Old rights come with getting a bigger share of the valley's overall water pie and having to pay a lot less per acre-foot. New rights mean less water and at a higher price."

"They're called senior rights. There are all sorts of water rights and laws to go with them. The stack of law books would fill a library. Surface rights, groundwater rights, prescriptive rights, appropriative rights, adjudicated rights. And then there are all the water contracts and water companies and irrigation districts and regulatory agencies to manage it all."

"I take it old Great-Grandpa Fabro had some of the first rights ever sold."

"He practically invented the allocation system." She yawned and arched her back. "All that wine is making me sleepy. I've been up since daybreak. Life as a farmer."

"And do the rights always stay with the land?"

"The simple answer? Unless you sell them or are forced to give them up."

"So whoever winds up with the most water winds up with the most money."

"If you put it that way, yes."

Jack stared out the window. The clouds had closed in and the sky was turning as dark as the residue of espresso that stained the bottom of the cup. "Tell me more about Jonathan Gossamer. What else do you know about him?"

"Does this mean you're going to help me?"

"Tell me about him first."

"I told you what I know. He called, he came, he threatened."

"What kind of threat did he make?"

She hesitated. "He's too smart to say anything. He lets you see him a couple of times then slithers away. You know he's there waiting but he doesn't rattle before he bites. Or in this case, shoots and tries to burn your cellar down."

"But the other guy, the bodyguard, he's no snake in the grass, is he?"

"He wants you to know he can strike anytime he wants."

"Tell me what your play is."

"What play? I'm not planning anything. I stopped doing that after Prague. I told you, everything is different now."

Grace took a deep breath and let it go. "I thought you wanted to help me. Help keep my husband alive, help save my winery. For God's sake, Jack, save me from being shot too. It's like you didn't hear a word I said."

"I heard you, all right. Loud and clear. I heard you say you've gone straight. I heard how you learned how to make wine and cook soup and decorate a house. You sound like you know what you're talking about so maybe it is true. Maybe you have left the life. But you're also talking about marrying a guy from a very wealthy family. You're talking about water rights that are worth a lot of money. You're talking about a guy willing to hurt people and cheat the system to get them. Those are the same traits in the marks we used to target."

He searched her face. "There are more winemakers in California than all the other states combined. You really expect me to believe Gossamer stumbled upon you by accident?"

"Accidents do happen. And I told you Stefan talked to other growers who've also been approached by Jonathan Gossamer. For all we know, he's already amassed a portfolio of water rights."

Jack held out the empty espresso cup as if it were a crossing guard's paddle. "Okay, say everything is true. You marry the man of your dreams. You're living the life you always wanted. You're happily digging in the dirt and along comes this snake and bites your husband. You take him to a hospital almost two hours away and who do you run into but the guy you ditched high and dry without so much as a Dear John, and now you ask him to help you. You said I'd understand if I knew why you left me, so here's your big chance."

Grace drew up her knees. Her shoulders rose and fell as she sucked in her breath and exhaled a whisper. "I was pregnant. I didn't know what else to do. You being you and me being me and doing what we were doing, it was all... all too much. I needed some space to sort things out."

"Mine?" He said it before he could check himself.

"See? That's exactly what I'm talking about. Of course yours."

He glanced around the room, retraced his steps since arriving. There were no signs of a child anywhere, no family portraits on the wall, framed snapshots on a shelf, no toys inside or out.

"I'm not asking for forgiveness, only understanding. Everything was so crazy back then. You know that. I guess I was a little crazy too. What I was doing. Remember how moody I used to get between jobs?" Grace shivered. "And when I found out I was pregnant, well, I had to get away. From you. From myself. From everything. You understand now, don't you?"

She bit her lip but it was no use. Her shoulders heaved and she hugged her legs to her chest and buried her face against her knees.

Outside the picture window the clouds began smashing into each other, sending spears of lightning hurtling toward the ground. Jack thought about leaving. He thought about staying. He thought about the life he and Grace once had. He thought about Henri in the ICU and the woman and child in the blurry photograph. He even thought about the damn dog. And then he thought about everything he and Katie were about to have. Past, present, and future. She was right. They all rolled together. And he'd been right too. His *'das-pa* just jumped up and took a huge bite.

Grace was rocking, still hugging her knees. She looked tired, defeated. It could have been an act but Jack couldn't tell. He gave her foot a gentle squeeze and watched as the rain fell from the sky as steadily as tears of regret.

7

D awn's silvery fingerprints were still visible as Jack exited the valley and headed west over Altamont Pass. The green hills were dotted with hundreds of huge wind turbines, their white blades spinning slowly. The freeway was already starting to swell with morning commuters, but he paid them little mind. The Citroën's radio was dialed to KCSM, a college station. A student DJ was at the controls and his tastes were firmly rooted in the kind of blue period of jazz that flourished long before he was born. He played Bill Evans and Thelonius Monk tracks back-to-back. "My Foolish Heart" nearly made Jack weep. "Straight No Chaser" made him want to slug somebody.

He caught a break crossing the Bay Bridge and sailed into the employees-only parking lot at The Pier Inn just in time for the waterfront dive's morning opening. The smell of grease warming on the griddle and stale beer from the night before greeted him as he took a stool. Wonder Boy was already at his usual station behind the bar. He filled a thick ceramic mug with coffee the viscosity of 30-weight and slid it in front of Jack.

"S-s-so how's Henri?" he said, trying to wrestle his elusive sibilants to ground.

Jack put both hands around the mug as if they needed warming. "Haven't seen him since you gave me the 411, but I'm on my way to the hospital now. A doctor is supposed to give us an update."

"S-s-stroke s-s-survivors who have a s-s-second within a year are two point s-s-seven five times less likely to s-s-survive. A myocardial infarction diminishes the chances by a factor of s-s-six." The statistician savant looked at his bar towel.

"Tell me something I don't know. Like, the odds the Giants are going to grab their fourth ring. The line on MadBum throwing two no-hitters this season. That the chances the Dodgers will blow another playoff exceed one hundred percent. Give me something I can smile about. Anything."

Wonder Boy went to work polishing the already spotless bar. He firmly believed the legend it was a plank from Sir Francis Drake's *Golden Hind*. "I have information on the name you s-s-sent me."

Jack straightened. "That fast? I only texted it a few hours ago. You do sleep, don't you?"

Wonder Boy didn't answer nor did he smile. No one had ever heard him laugh. He never talked about his personal life. He was even more guarded about the names and contact numbers of every snitch, gossip, and rumormonger he kept in his head. The only thing the regulars at the Pier knew was he worked seven days a week and occasionally could be spotted sitting alone at a Giants game logging ERAs, WHIPs, WARs, BB/K ratios, and all the other equations that made America's pastime a true thinking person's game.

"Anonymity is difficult with s-s-such an unusual name as Jonathan Gossamer," Wonder Boy finally said. "He's left a trail as s-s-shiny as a s-s-snail's."

Jack lifted the coffee mug. "When Grace Millefiore gave it to me, I pictured one of those online companies with two stuffy English surnames separated by an ampersand to hide the fact it's actually two punks in dirty hoodies living in a trailer park in Milpitas."

"He's the managing partner of a hedge fund, Wine Futures, Inc. It's headquartered here in S-s-san Francisco."

"I knew people invested in rare vintages like they do antiques and fine art, but now there's a market in stuff that hasn't even been bottled yet? What'll they think of next."

Wonder Boy took Jack's breakfast order and poured more coffee. He rearranged the liquor bottles so all the labels faced exactly outward.

Jack went to work on the pair of sunny sides that rested atop a bed of hash browns before asking, "What more can you tell me about Wine Futures?"

"Their investment s-s-strategy is vertical as well as horizontal. Brands, vineyards, bottlers, wholesalers, and distributors. They even have a s-s-stake in a graphic artist who designs labels. They package these into funds for clients. They charge the s-s-standard hedge fund two and twenty. Two percent management fee plus twenty percent performance fee."

"How about water? More specifically, water rights belonging to the growers. Are those in their funds?"

"It's not featured in their offering prospectus nor in their S-S-SEC filing forms. The company is s-s-so new it doesn't have last year's tax form on file yet. Only a couple of estimated quarterlies."

Jack didn't ask Wonder Boy how he'd obtained those because that would violate the rules. "What about the man himself? Does he have any history?"

"No criminal s-s-sheet that I could find but I only s-s-searched domestically."

"All that means is he's never been caught. What else?"

"The company's website has a short bio. It s-s-says he was born in Connecticut, went to Choate prep s-s-school, undergrad at Dartmouth, and earned an MBA at Business S-s-school Lausanne. That's in S-s-switzerland."

"Any legit jobs?"

"The bio lists one year at Goldman S-s-sachs in Manhattan before transferring to their S-s-san Francisco office. He left after three months and founded Wine Futures. S-s-so he's been here about a year all together."

"Sounds like a made-up cover. Jonathan Gossamer. The more the syllables, the more likely the alias."

"I'd s-s-say s-s-so."

"How old is he?"

"Twenty s-s-seven."

Jack whistled. "Kids these days, what you going do?"

He ate some more eggs and potatoes. "Grace says he never goes anywhere without muscle. She didn't have a name. Did you find anything on who he uses for security?"

"No, but I can put out s-s-some feelers."

"Okay but on the QT. We don't want to flush him yet."

"Understood."

"You have an address for this Jonathan Gossamer?"

"His office is in the Pacific Tower on S-s-sansome S-s-street. A s-s-suite on the fifteenth floor."

Jack nearly stabbed himself with the fork. "On the corner of California?"

"S-s-southeast. Do you know it?"

"Yeah. Lots of private financial consultants and wealth managers have offices there, the kind that don't put names on the lobby marquee. It's expensive real estate. It's also on the same corner where Henri had his heart attack."

JACK TRIED CALLING Alison and Ji-min again as he crossed China Basin and drove up to Potrero Avenue. Neither nurse picked up and so he left voicemails asking to return his call ASAP. He found a stall on the third floor of the medical center parking garage and took the stairway down to street level. The homeless were still encamped in the common areas of SF General and Jack avoided the cafeteria as if the day's special was bubonic plague au gratin.

Katie wasn't the only one sitting in the ICU's cramped waiting room. Hark was thumbing through a dog-eared *Highlights*. "Who brings a kid to visit someone in the ICU?" he said. "And who fills in all the puzzles in ink?"

Jack sat beside Katie and put his arm around her. "Have you talked to the doctor yet?"

"He's with Henri now."

Hark looked up. "You met the nurse? The tall one? She's, uh, she's something."

"You falling in love again?" Jack said.

Hark's neck tat rippled. His given name was Geraldo but the inker had misspelled it as Herald. That and the angel wings gave rise to his handle. "Don't bring that up, okay? Moana like to break my heart when she moved back to Tonga."

Katie patted the big man on the knee and then turned to Jack. "Were you able to help Grace fix her plumbing problems?"

Hark sounded as if he swallowed something down the wrong pipe. Jack ignored him. "It's going to take some time. It's complicated."

"That's a term people use to describe their relationship status on social media," Katie said archly.

"Hey, babe, I'm the one who called last night and told you it wasn't safe to drive home, what with the rain coming down so hard and, well, after a few glasses of vino. Nothing happened, if that's what's you're thinking."

"I wasn't thinking anything of the sort." She suddenly looked pleased with herself.

Jack squinted and then decided he had no chance of figuring out what was behind the smile.

Hark recovered from his choking fit. "So, *vato*, you find anything more about what Henri was doing in the city?"

"I've only talked to one of his private nurses. I'm still trying to connect with the other two. There was some stuff in his, uh, desk, that still needs running down."

"Sounds like you need help. Count me in."

"I could use it."

Swinging doors from the ICU swished open and a man in green scrubs followed by Taylor S. entered the waiting room. Jack stood. Katie did too. Hark stayed seated but rolled up the magazine as if preparing to swat a fly.

"I wish I could be more reassuring," the doctor said in a clipped tone. "Mr. LeConte remains in grave condition. While brain monitoring shows activity—and in some quarters that could be viewed as a positive—he remains dependent on a ventilator and external heart stimulator. It's my opinion he's unlikely to get off either unless something dramatic happens. The question you have to ask yourself is what would he want? I understand you're his conservator, Mr. McCoul, but there's no health directive on file."

"It's probably in his safe deposit box. I have the key but I need to run down which branch."

The doctor gave him a disapproving look before leaving. Taylor S. rolled her eyes. "I'd apologize for ol' Dr. Braveheart but they don't pay me near enough to do his PR too. Cardiologists, you'd think they'd have big ones. Hearts, I'm talking about." She flashed some teeth at Hark. He smiled right back. "Surgeons can be even colder. You know the joke. Robots are going to replace them in the OR but no one will ever notice." She heh-heh-heh'ed. So did Hark.

"Can we go in and see Henri now?" Katie asked.

"Of course but only two at a time. Ward policy. I'll take you."

Hark stayed seated. "You all go. I'll wait here." He unrolled the *Highlights*.

Jack's phone buzzed before he could move. The number flashing on caller ID belonged to one of the student nurses. "I got to take this," he told Katie. "You go ahead. I'll catch up in a second."

He waited until Taylor S. and Katie were gone before picking up. "Alison? It's Jack McCoul. Thanks for returning my call."

"You sure about that?" a man responded.

Jack recognized the voice right off. "Excuse me but who is this?"

"Don't play stupid. You know who it is."

"Terry? What are you doing with this phone?"

"How about you tell me?" Lieutenant Terrence Dolan countered. "I'm in an apartment on Clement Street. There's a dead woman with a plastic bag taped over her head and a phone underneath the pillow. I check the messages. You sounded pretty desperate to reach her. Then I hit redial and now you're pretending it's a big joke."

Jack had a rule of always starting with the truth when talking to a homicide cop. "The word is *persistent* not *desperate*. I never met her. All I know is she's a nurse. She's been tending to a friend of mine. Now he's in a coma at SF General. I called to let her know."

"I'm going to need more than that. A lot more. Names. Details. Your whereabouts at TOD once the coroner establishes it."

"Sounds official. I better run your request by Cicero Broadshank. You know how my attorney is about cops abiding by the rules."

Terry didn't bite. "You say your friend is in a coma?"

"That's right. In fact, I'm with him at the hospital right now."

"Then he won't know you've left."

"Who's says I'm going anywhere?"

"I am. You're coming here for starters. After that, we'll see."

"And why would I want to do that?"

"Because it'll save the city the cost of me sending a couple of uniforms to arrest you for obstruction and you having to pay Broadshank to bail you out."

"Settle down." Jack gave it a couple of beats. Another one of his rules was always keep a cop off balance, especially one still carrying a torch. "Let me tell Katie. She's here too. She's getting her prenatal checkup."

The phone going dead in his hand was cause for a grin.

8

They took Hark's car. The '64 lowrider earned plenty of signs flashed by street corner wannabes as they cut through the Mission. Hark acknowledged the show of respect by gunning the V-8. Twin chrome tail pipes connected to Flowmasters spit flames and roared. He palmed the chain link steering wheel as they turned onto Castro Street. Brightly painted Victorians lined both sides. Jack stared out the window from his shotgun perch in the tuck 'n roll bucket and ran through what he knew and didn't. The "didn't column" took three times as long.

"Give it to me again," Hark said. "Henri has three nurses. You talked to one, you can't reach another, and now the third one's dead."

"That's about the size of it."

"Wonder what Wonder Boy would say the odds are she had a bad date. Or maybe it was a second-story man come through her bedroom window and doesn't want to leave a witness. He happening to bring a plastic bag to carry away the loot. This being not anything to do with Henri."

"Hundred to one," Jack said. "Not even."

A giant rainbow flag waved proudly at the intersection of Market Street despite the wet weather. They passed through Duboce Triangle, Castro turning into Divisadero on the north side. A couple of soul food restaurants still hung on in the Western Addition despite the relentless march of gentrification.

"So fess up, *ese*. What the hell were you thinking going to Grace's crib and spending the night? Or is it like what I said, the witch still casting spells on you."

"I've been asking myself the same thing. You think you can leave stuff behind but it has a way of hitchhiking no matter how careful you check your luggage." He drummed his fingers on the door panel. "Grace and her husband got themselves sideways with some player who's making moves on the water market. His name is Jonathan Gossamer. She asked me to help for old time's sake. That's all there is between us. Nothing more."

"That's good. Better than good seeing she's never exactly been the healthiest for your health. Not like Katie is, all due respect. This player. What's his name again?"

"Jonathan Gossamer."

"This Goss dude, he the one shot Grace's old man?"

"More likely he had his hired gun do it. Grace says Gossamer never goes anywhere without him, a real life Chia Pet."

"You mean he's so stone cold the only way you know he's alive is his hair grows. What did he use for the hit?"

Jack told him.

"That's some shooting. Twenty-two's pretty light to strap much of a night scope on. Suppose he could've been using NV goggles." He thought on it some. "When I was in the 'Stan, snipers were a breed apart. Kept to themselves and didn't mix. And that was fine with me. You wanted them all up in themselves when you were on patrol, hiding the way they do, shooting the way they do. Talk about eyes in the sky. Better than drones. There was this one dude, a hillbilly type. He gave me some pointers on how to put one smack middle in the forehead from a klick away. Course he used a Barrett .50 cal mounted on a tripod. Still."

"Gossamer's triggerman isn't some local deer hunter. He sounds like the type who gets top dollar for protecting rich folks. Gossamer probably writes it off on his taxes as overhead."

"Most of the dudes in that line of work either were in the man's army or did stints as mercs." Hark worked his jaw. "I know a place they call their own. Maybe I can find out who's working for your player. Better it's me checking it out than you. On account of my time over there."

"Don't forget to show them the scars, wear your Purple Heart."

Hark grinned.

Jack said, "There's more."

"What kind of more?"

"Henri's heart attack? He had it in front of Gossamer's office."

"*Chingame.*"

"And the dead nurse? She was supposed to be with Henri that day."

"Fuck me."

They took Geary Boulevard up to the Richmond District and jogged a block over to Clement Street. Every other storefront was a restaurant, most of them Chinese. Thai was also big.

"There," Jack said as they crossed Ninth. "That's Terry's Crown Vic blocking the driveway up ahead. Looks like the CSI meat wagon is still there too."

"I'll drop you. The joint I want to check out is back over on Geary. I'll see what's up and catch you later."

Two floors of apartments were stacked above a street-level

storefront that was divided between a mom-and-pop hardware store and a sports bar with an overly cute sign advertising fifty-seven varieties of beer. A beat cop blocked the stairwell. Jack told him his name. The cop hooked a thumb.

"There's a box of paper booties. They go on your feet." He smelled like he'd been sampling freebies from the Korean barbeque joint across the street.

The top floor landing was crowded with investigative equipment and people who made a living from murders. There were four apartments. The pulse of hip-hop playing from behind a closed door made the hall lamp jiggle. Another door was festooned with political bumper stickers dating back to the '80s.

One door was open. Lieutenant Terrence Dolan was standing in the middle of the living room, talking on the phone. He was dressed for success as he always was: a navy blue suit, crisp white shirt, and a rep tie with colors as muted as his expression. He held up a cautioning finger, finished the call with an abrupt, "I need it within the hour." He pointed the phone at Jack as if it were a gun.

"You didn't tell me your sick friend is Henri LeConte."

"You didn't ask."

"Ask you for the time of day and you have to think about what's in it for you. Some things never change."

"Like your goal of becoming they city's youngest chief in history, no matter who you step on climbing up the ladder? I hear you got promoted to lieutenant since last I saw you."

"What's LeConte's relationship to the victim?"

"I told you. She's his nurse. He's her patient."

"How do you know that? You said you've never met her."

It was a weak *gotcha* and Jack swatted it away easily. "Henri keeps a scheduler on his refrigerator with dates and names. Alison's Mondays, Tuesdays, and Thursdays. Was, I should say. Don't take my word for it. Call the College of Marin. She's a nursing student there. They have a job center. You'll have to find out what her last name is yourself. It wasn't on Henri's list."

"Kanasis."

"As I said, I didn't know. I've never met her."

"Well, here's your chance."

Jack knew Terry was going for shock and awe, and though he'd seen dead bodies before, he'd never gotten used to it. He followed the cop into the bedroom. The curtains to the bay windows were pulled aside. Daylight shined on the bed but didn't lighten the body any. It was already bloated and blue. Green blotches spread across the abdomen where millions of microorganisms still alive in the gut were busy breaking down dead cells. The plastic bag duct taped around the student nurse's neck was fogged like a car window with no defroster.

The cop eyed Jack carefully. "You still going to keep with your story?"

"Stick to the truth. You don't have to remember the parts you made up. Mark Twain."

A pair of crime scene workers in matching white Tyvek suits came in. One carried a folded black body bag. "You ready for us, LT?"

"Yes and leave the window open. They'll close it when they seal the front door."

Jack followed him back to the living room. He stopped clamping his nose but the smell wouldn't go away.

Terry squared up to him. "You said she was Mondays, Tuesdays, and Thursdays. How many others names are on the schedule?"

"Two. I spoke to one. Her name is Rainey. Wednesdays and Fridays. No last name listed either. She didn't know Henri had a heart attack. I called the other one as many times as I called Alison but no contact yet. Her name is Ji-min."

"Saturdays and Sundays. You got an address for her?"

"Nope. Just the phone number. Rainey said she thought she lived in the Marina but wasn't positive. The college should have it."

"Give me the other two nurses' numbers."

"I'll text you the list. I snapped a photo of it."

"You took quite an interest trying to reach these ladies. Seems unusual."

"Henri's unusual," Jack fired back. "He's old school. He'd want them to know. I was doing it for him. Just like I'm taking care of his dog. Just like I'm helping you."

The cop's expression showed the dig hit home. "Henri LeConte's nothing but another career criminal."

"Allegedly. We done here?"

"For now."

Jack turned to leave. He hadn't reached the door before the homicide detective said, "When did LeConte have the heart attack?"

"Monday."

"Alison's day according to your so-called schedule."

"That's right."

"Then she would've known he had it."

"*If* she was with him, but the EMT report didn't mention it. Why I was calling her. Anything else?"

"If this Ji-min calls you before I get ahold of her, your next call better be to me."

"Sure, Terry. Want me to say hi to Katie for you? I'm on my way to pick her up and take her out for ice cream. She's got the cravings."

9

It was five and dinner was being served on SF General's fourth floor. Some of the doors to the private rooms were open, and Jack glanced in as he passed down the hall. They resembled hotel suites, and the soothing paint colors and homey furnishings were the design equivalent of a dose of Valium. Jack wondered if the open wards assigned to the city's indigent had the look of Thorazine. He stopped outside Room 425. The door was closed. Determining the muffled voices were coming from a television, he entered without knocking.

"Stefan Fabro?"

"What now?" The patient was propped up in bed with a silver IV stand on one side and a moveable overbed table with an untouched bowl of Jell-O on the other. "If I have to state my birthday one more time, I'll go nuts. Do you know how many times a day I'm asked? Even when they bring in the commode, I can't do my business until I say it."

"Don't worry, I'm not with the hospital."

"Are you the insurance adjustor then? I spent an hour on the phone with your home office, trying to sort this out. The policy's supposed to cover everything except the deductible."

"Your wife told me you're here. I have a friend in the ICU and thought I'd stop by to say hello before going there."

"What did you say your name is?"

"Jack McCoul."

If it registered, Fabro didn't show it. He had the build of someone used to tilling fields and hoisting barrels of wine. A week in the hospital made his tan look jaundiced and the bags under his eyes were the color of bruised bananas.

"How do you know Grace?" he asked.

"From back in the day. San Francisco's a small town. You grow up here, sooner or later you run into everyone. How you feeling?"

"Ready to go home. Don't get me wrong, the people here saved my life. And they're trying hard with the food too. They even let me have wine with dinner. Well, a half glass anyway. Grace sneaks some of ours in."

"I tried it. It's very good."

"We've earned some good reviews and more and more high-end restaurants are featuring it. Where did you find it? A store or restaurant?"

"Your place. Grace had me out for a tour and lunch." He toed the door closed and approached the bed. "She told me about the water. She told me about Jonathan Gossamer and his bodyguard."

Fabro winced. "Are you a policeman?"

"I'm a friend of your wife's. I'm concerned for her safety."

Red overtook yellow in Fabro's cheeks. "Who says I'm not? I filed a report. I gave the sheriff's department what they asked for. They're investigating."

"Even if they are, they're not equipped to deal with something like this."

"What do you know?"

"I've got experience with people like Gossamer."

"I can handle this myself. My family has been in the valley for generations. We still know plenty of people in high places. A couple of state senators, the head of California Department of Food and Ag. Half the members on the water commission. All I have to do is pick up the phone."

"Trust me, you're going to need a lot more muscle than a Sacramento bureaucrat."

Fabro punched the air. It stretched the IV tube and nearly pulled the stand over. "Grace and I aren't about to be pushed off our land by some shyster with a business card. We're not going to give up what's rightfully ours without a fight. We've worked too hard."

"You're in way over your head and you don't even know it."

"I'm going to ask you to leave now."

"Fine but don't fool yourself into thinking you can solve this on your own or it will go away. There's too much money at stake. And the people you're up against?" Jack grimaced. "If you love your wife, then hire someone to guard your house. Next time they won't bother hiding among the vines."

"I'm sorry, handsome. Nothing's changed." Taylor S. made a clucking noise. "You can go on in but only for a few minutes. We're right up against closing time. ICU rules."

"Thanks but I want to ask you something first," Jack said.

"Sure, anything. And by the way, congratulations, daddy-to-be. Your wife told me. She also told me it's okay I still call you handsome as long as it doesn't go to your head. You're lucky. She's something."

"Don't I know it."

"What do you need?"

"It's about Henri's personal effects. His clothes and wallet and such. You said the EMTs brought him to the ER and later he was transferred up here. Is his stuff still downstairs?"

The nurse's bouffant swayed back and forth. "Supposed to be right here. A patient's belongings follow the patient no matter where in the hospital they're transferred. Their things get put in a clear bag with a patient ID sticker stuck on it. Same as the one on their bracelet. If they're in a room, the bag goes in the closet. If they're in a ward like the ICU here, it goes in a cubby. There's a wall of them in the staff room over there. I don't recall putting it away but, hey, they don't pay me enough to work every shift. Is there something special in it?"

"I'm hoping he had his address book with him. There's people I should notify."

She winked. "And maybe there's something in his wallet that will give you an idea where that safe deposit box you mentioned to Dr. Heartless is."

"Taylor, I could kiss you."

"Ah, don't do that. I'd spoil you. Now if that big friend of yours wants to, well, tell him that would be all right with me. Go on, then. Door's open. The cubby's have the patient's names written on the front."

Jack found Henri's. He placed the bag of clothes on a dining table and pulled out the items one at a time. Henri had been wearing a blue and charcoal windowpane sport jacket, pleated gray flannel slacks, and a gold and turquoise silk ascot with a matching pocket kerchief. His belt and capped-toe Oxfords also matched. The socks were midcalf and his boxers had broad stripes and a button fly.

A leather glasses case was in the jacket's right inside breast pocket. Jack opened it. The bifocals had alligator frames. There was nothing else in the case. Henri's wallet was in the left inside breast pocket. It contained $600 in cash: four $100 bills and ten $20s. The Benjamins were crisp but they had an old secretary of treasury's signature. Plastic was limited to a credit card and a bank debit card. Henri's driver's license featured an unusually good portrait. Jack guessed he'd made the ID himself.

Tucked in a fold was an ATM receipt for $200. That accounted for the ten Jacksons. It was dated the same morning he'd had the heart attack. Jack looked closely and could make out the bank's address. He knew it. The lobby doubled as a California history museum, a favorite stop for tourists interested in gold rush memorabilia. It was also next to the Pacific Tower.

10

Seven shades of gray layered over San Francisco Bay. Squalls blew in through Golden Gate, and Jack watched graphite clouds with flat bottoms skate over turbulent water the color of slate as he walked Chagall along the Crissy Field promenade. The usually busy shoreline park that stretched from the Marina to the bridge was nearly empty and the blustery weather and lateness of the day was a deterrent for all but the most diehard of adrenaline junkies.

Jack urged the dog forward. "We're not going back until you lift a leg."

The shaggy poodle ignored him as he nosed the many scents along the trail. They crossed a footbridge over a lagoon. A great blue heron and several egrets hunkered along the marshy edges. Even the patches of beach strawberry and sticky monkeyflower in the dunes seemed to be lying lower than usual as the wind sprayed everything in its path with a stinging mix of salt and sand.

Chagall finally found inspiration at a fence post, and with mission accomplished, Jack returned to the parking lot. The Citroën was no longer alone. Hark's customized Chevy idled right alongside. Jack put the dog in the back seat of the French sedan before joining his friend.

"Wet dog's going stink up Henri's whip something fierce," Hark said. "We had to reupholster a '73 Monaco once on account the owner always let his pit ride shotgun."

"Tell me about it. Katie's burning scented candles and they're still not up to the job."

"Riders on the Storm" was playing on the lowrider's sound system. Jack could feel the *thwomp* of the subwoofer in the trunk.

"Good choice," he said.

"I got a playlist of weather oldies but goldies. Dylan's "Hard Rain," Martha's "Heat Wave." Even got Neil Young's "Like a Hurricane." The live version. But the stuff going on out there?" He jabbed a finger at the windshield. "It's got Jim Morrison written all over it."

"Into this world we're thrown, Like a dog without a bone." Jack delivered a pretty good imitation.

He listened to the rest of the track before continuing. "Did you get some intel from your tent mates?"

"It's like you thought," Hark said. "This dude Goss hired is a pro. He got his training courtesy of *Tio* Sam. His name is Tully. He was an operator in Afghanistan. After that, he did private security over there for the big Texas companies who locked up all the logistics contracts. You know, building the camps, running the cargo trucks, supplying the chow. They're the ones who made a killing off both wars."

"How long has Tully been with Gossamer?"

"About a year as far as anybody here knows but I'm not so sure his boss has been around much longer than that anyway."

Jack told him that's what Wonder Boy had discovered too. "What else did you learn?"

"Tully's got a rep. Ninety-nine percent of Special Ops dudes are, no doubt about it, heroes. But every barrel, well, you know. Word is somewhere along the way he stepped over the line, and they couldn't pull him back. Something about being on a night raid deep inside and he didn't care who he shot when the lights went down and the shit hit. After a couple of more like that, he mustered out or more likely they mustered him out, and he went into the have gun will travel business."

"Sounds like he's the sort of bad news the censors at Facebook pull. If he were taking aim at Grace's husband, he wouldn't've missed unless he meant to. Probably just sending a message."

"Pretty stout message." Hark fiddled with the controls on his music player. "He's got to have himself a partner too. Someone driving the pickup truck and heaving the Molotov. Goss, Tully, and a third dude. Three little bears. Or is it three little pigs? I can never remember."

"We need to even the odds. Can you find a couple of guys who can pull double duty at Grace's vineyard? Blend in as field hands by day and guards at night?"

"You think Goss will have Tully take another run at it?"

"I talked to Grace's husband. He's going to be released from the hospital any day now but he's in no shape to fend off anyone."

"His wounds that bad?"

"He'll heal but he's out of his league. He wouldn't know where to look for the right kind of help even if he admitted he needed it. Forget Tully having his lunch, Stefan wouldn't make it past breakfast."

Hark thought on it some. "There some low lows I know live over in Modesto. They'd do it for a price."

"If you trust them I trust them. Reach out and when you confirm it, I'll tell Grace to expect some company."

"You find anything more on Goss?"

"I'm on my way to get a first look now. There's a fundraiser at the Fairmont and Wine Futures is listed on the flyer as a sponsor. I'm betting he'll be there."

"If you're planning on calling him out, I better go with you. Have your back because Tully will have his."

"You take outside, I'll take inside. I only want to see how he works people. I don't want him to ID me. Best to leave our options open in case this comes down to needing a different sort of resolution."

Hark slapped the steering wheel. "That's what I'm talking about, *vato*. Time to come out of retirement."

"It'd be good to find out where Gossamer lives. I only have his office address."

"I'll tail him when they're done partying."

"Let's meet up out front and see if we can catch a glimpse when they arrive."

Jack opened the door and slid out of the Impala as the Allman Brothers' "Stormy Monday" began playing. Hark cranked up the volume and the guitar riffs and lyrics echoed in the gloaming as he eased away.

THE FAIRMONT HOTEL commanded a prime perch atop Nob Hill. The first time Tony Bennett crooned "I Left My Heart in San Francisco," he was clutching a microphone in the Venetian Room. The Tonga Room downstairs was one of the oldest tiki bars in America, its signature hurricane cocktails clocking in at 250 calories per drink.

Jack and Hark sat on a bench in Huntington Park right across from the main entrance. Cars approached in single file for the valet drop-off. Jack downloaded a photo of Jonathan Gossamer from the Wine Futures website onto his phone and was checking it against the arrivals. Teslas and Audis were the vehicles of choice for the hoi polloi. A black Lincoln crossover pulled up and Jack made the match when the passenger stepped out.

Jonathan Gossamer was slight with a thin face and wore his frosted hair high and tight. He had on a trendy slim-cut blazer over an untucked white dress shirt and no tie. A pair of red Pumas provided a dash of color. He looked young, confident, and successful. The driver exited without acknowledging the valet. He had a close-cropped beard and was dressed in a dark jacket and dark shirt.

"That must be Tully," Hark said. They watched him round the car quickly. Gossamer was waiting for him and fell in behind as his bodyguard led the way. "Look, he's walking point like he's back in Helmand Province. And that bulge on his hip is no wallet."

The valet got in the driver's seat of the Lincoln and pulled away from the entrance.

Hark said, "Isn't that the model that actor drives? You know, the dude in those TV ads where you don't know what he's talking about. Drives with the sunroof open when it's raining. Jumps in a pool with a tuxedo on."

"About how you got to go backwards to go forward. That's what he's saying."

"You mean his transmission's out? He bring it around to my shop, I'll fix it for him."

"Lower it a few inches and put some metal flake in the paint job while you're at it."

"You got that right."

Jack said, "I'm going in to do some recon of our boys. When you find out where they call home, give a call."

"Roger that."

Jack made his way to the Grand Ballroom. He blended right

in. San Francisco being San Francisco, the attire ranged from blue jeans to black tie. The master of ceremonies was the crusty head of the state Democratic Party, a retired congressman who favored aloha shirts and peppered his remarks with four-letter words.

Jack snagged a glass of wine from a tray carried by a server who wore her SEIU hotel workers badge proudly and joined the circulating crowd. He let the rotational force carry him until he spotted his quarry. Gossamer was holding forth in the room's nucleus, chatting amiably with the city's power elite. Among them were the mayor, the CEOs of some of the biggest tech companies in the world as well as a smattering of billionaires turned activists. Clusters of local elected officials, trial lawyers, campaign managers, and PR flacks orbited nearby.

Jack kept watch for Tully as he circulated but never saw him. When he was directly behind Gossamer he allowed the crowd's Coriolis effect to deposit him among a group of hangers-on who were hoping to be sucked into the black hole of exclusivity. Jack smiled and pretended to be interested while catching snatches of Gossamer's conversation.

The moguls listening to him had a combined personal net worth that would put them among the top 100 countries ranked by GNP. Gossamer was telling them about a recent head-to-head competition between a French 1990 Chateau Haut-Brion Bordeaux and a Napa 1990 Heitz Cabernet Sauvignon. He licked his lips when talking. He segued effortlessly to the contents of a personal cellar he recently obtained at a private auction. His message was subtle but clear: He was willing to bestow a few trophy vintages for his new friends, a free sample for the hedge funds he really wanted to sell them.

Jack edged closer for a personal gut check. He was a quick read of people but his internal radar system served as the ultimate test. It rarely let him down when it came to distinguishing threat from opportunity, undercover cop from mark. But a loud disruption broke out near the entrance to the ballroom before he got a chance. Voices shouted and placards waved. A group of vegans were screaming for an end to meat and dairy products. "Free the cheese," they shouted. "All cows are sacred." Hotel security guards scrambled to prevent the party crashers from gaining any more ground. Tully was at Jonathan Gossamer's side in an instant. He'd been using the crowd as camouflage just as Jack had. He guided his charge toward a fire exit without causing so much as a ripple among the sea of VIPs.

Jack didn't need his gut to tell him Tully was a pro when it came to sneaking in and sneaking out. He also didn't need it to tell him that the hired gun's experience extended beyond performing live extractions in the dead of night.

11

The sun made an entrance the next morning. The downtown skyscrapers looked shiny and the streets around them freshly scrubbed. So did Jack. He was shaved, showered, and suited up. His tie with brown kangaroos on it was knotted, his loafers polished, his wig combed. He was everything a well-dressed estate executor should look like. He was going to scam a bank.

At 9:00 am sharp he pushed through the glass doors, limped past a red stagecoach pulled by a team of life-size plastic horses, and patted one on the rump. An officious young man stationed in the middle of the marble-floored lobby greeted him with a smile.

"May I help you, sir?"

Jack pushed the bridge of his black-framed cheaters. "G'day. A senior manager, if you please. I require release documents for an estate I represent."

"Certainly, sir. This way, if you please."

Jack limped behind him toward a covey of oak desks separated by low partitions. Each desk sported a brass nameplate. Amal Singh was sitting behind his. He gave a perfunctory bow.

"How may I be of service?"

"G'day. Name's Finnimore. I've been appointed executor of one of your customer's estate. A Mr. Henri LeConte, recently deceased." Jack raised his briefcase. "I got the necessary documents right here in my port. We'll be leaving his cash and investment accounts as is till we finish paying off his obligations, but according to his wishes, we're to disperse his personal items matched to a list of recipients ASAP. Family and mates, mainly." He patted his leg. "Great white nipped me while I was surfing at Bondi Beach. Mind if I have a seat?"

"Sorry, sir. Of course."

"No worries." Jack opened the case, pulled out a labeled accordion file, and extracted documents he'd spent the evening printing: a signed and sealed death certificate, a last will and testament with a three-year-old date on it, and a spiral-bound seventy-eight page document with the logo of a well-known law firm prominently displayed on the cover. The title read "Henri LeConte Revocable Trust."

"I'll need proof of my visit for the estate's records as well as access to the decedent's safety deposit box to retrieve his personal effects," he said.

Singh's suit was a size too big. "Certainly." He clicked away on his keyboard. "LeConte, Henri. Yes, I found his accounts but we don't have him listed as deceased. In fact, I see by the records he signed into his safe deposit box last Monday."

Jack pushed over the death certificate. "You can copy that but I'm afraid I'll need it back. Somehow I got out of the office with only the one. My assistant can send you over one."

The banker's hair was thinning on top. "I can scan it right here. All records are digital now. Naturally, I will need to see proof of identification."

Jack handed over an Australian driver's license and passport.

The banker studied them. "So you are from Sydney, Mr. Finnimore?"

"That's right but I've been in Frisco three months now. The firm's got me running since I hit the ground, I'll tell you. Haven't even had a chance to find a flat yet. Staying at the Hyatt, I am." He screwed up his face. "I got to say what the landlords are getting away with makes Circular Quay back home seem cheap and that's no slouch of a neighborhood either."

"The demand is high but so is employment," Singh said diplomatically. "You should be aware there is a modest charge for the bank providing notary services. I'm a notary so we can do it right here. We can debit the estate's checking account. Do you have a key to the box or will you require the services of a locksmith?"

Jack held up a sterling silver key ring he'd purchased at the Fairmont's gift shop the night before. Dangling from it was the key he'd removed from Henri's bombé chest. "No worries. Got it right here."

Jack signed everything with his own pen and carefully returned it to his pocket. He limped behind Singh to the vault. A wall of bronze boxes stacked floor to head high gleamed under the florescent lights. The banker found Box 1405 and inserted the master key. Jack handed him his key. The lock opened and the banker removed a long metal box. He glanced at Jack's leg.

"It is not heavy, Mr. Finnimore, however, I would be happy to carry it to a private room for you if you wish."

"That'd be grand."

Singh placed it on a table in a small enclosure and closed the door when he left. Jack slipped on a pair of latex gloves. The box would be the only thing he left behind. He lifted the lid. Good old Henri. Jack could see a banded stack of crisp Benjamins that were the same vintage as the ones he'd found in the old art forger's wallet along with the ATM receipt. They were $100 breadcrumbs. Next to them was a note written on a deposit slip. The handwriting was shaky.

"If you're reading this, then you're as smart as I always knew you were and I'm probably as dead as I was always going to be. Damn ticker is acting up, *mon fils*. I know you'll do what needs doing. *Au voire,* Henri."

Beneath the note was a purple envelope. Jack lifted it by the corners as if it were parchment. It was addressed to Henri in flowing cursive. The return had no name, only a San Francisco post office box number but no zip code. The date was smudged. The envelope had been slit open. There was no note inside, only three snapshots.

The top one was the original of the photocopy he already had. It was in much sharper focus. Jack studied the image closely. The woman's dress was simple, her raven hair brushed but not styled. Her skin tone was brown, her eyes dark. The expression she wore was indecipherable, neither happy nor sad. Jack turned his focus on the child. She was simply dressed too. There was nothing about the setting or the condition of the photo that gave any indication of the year. It could be from weeks ago or decades past.

The second photo was of the little girl playing in what appeared to be a front yard. The corner of a house peeked behind foliage and beyond that was the blue haze of distant mountains. His gut told him they weren't the Sierra Nevada.

The third photo was a close-up of the little girl. He could see something shiny in her hair. It was a silver barrette. She seemed to be staring back at him, and he could not blink away the look in her blue eyes. It belonged to someone older, someone who had seen both sides of life, both the good and the bad, love and disappointment.

He fanned the three photos on the table next to the metal safety deposit box so he could study them together. They offered more questions than answers. He slid them back into the envelope and slipped it in his jacket pocket. There was nothing more in the box so he closed the lid and called for Singh to place it back in the vault.

THE N-JUDAH CLATTERED WEST OUT of the Sunset Tunnel and into a daylight mottled by puffy clouds. The light rail's first stop was Carl at Cole. Jack got off. He'd traded the suit for his usual jeans and leather jacket but still felt like the man as he walked through the Haight. At least a building a block sported a purple paint job and '60s peace symbols hung in more than a few windows. The kids on the street were three generations removed from the Summer of Love but tie-dye and Jerry Garcia T-shirts appeared never to have gone out of style.

Six stairs led to the front door of a Queen Anne that had survived the 1906 earthquake but was now in danger of collapsing from landlord neglect. The paint job was peeling and the bay windows were in desperate need of new caulk. A row of intercom buttons with names handwritten below them signaled it had been divided into apartments. Jack pushed #5.

"Yes?" a shaky voice answered.

"It's Jack McCoul. You called, I came. You want to let me in?"

"Are you alone?"

"Look out the window and see for yourself."

The buzzer buzzed and the automatic lock clicked and Jack entered a darkened lobby that smelled of mildew. Discarded Amazon boxes were piled in one corner. A vase on a lopsided table held plastic flowers that appeared stolen from a cemetery. The stairs were wooden and Jack's footsteps made drumbeats as he climbed to the second floor. He knocked and smiled at the peephole.

Rainey was dressed in black yoga pants and a gray sweater. Her hair could use a shampoo. She was holding her hand to her throat and her red plastic glasses needed straightening. When Jack closed the door behind him, she double-checked the lock.

"I'm scared out of my mind. The detective said Alison was strangled. He said they can't find Ji-min. I've called her too. She hasn't called me back." She whimpered. "Oh my god, I could be next."

Jack sucked his teeth and looked around the room. It was furnished by Craigslist. Jane Austen dominated the rickety bookshelf. "You're jumping to conclusions. As cops go, Lieutenant Dolan's good at what he does. He'll find who did it."

"How do you know?"

"Dolan's earned a reputation for always getting his man or woman. Look, if he thought you were in any danger, he wouldn't have left you here. What happened to Alison could have nothing to do with Ji-min being hard to reach. Maybe she took a trip. Maybe she forgot to pay her phone bill."

"I'm not stupid. The detective asked me about Henri. There's a connection all right."

"What kind of questions?"

"How long I worked for him. What did I know about him. Did I know about his heart attack before you called me. Where was I on Wednesday." Rainey shuddered.

"Anything else?"

"He asked, like, a million questions. Ugh. When was the last time I saw Alison. Did she have a boyfriend. Did she talk about anybody, say anything about somebody who was mad at her or anything. What did I know about you. That sort of thing. I can't remember it all."

"What did you tell Dolan about me?"

"Only that I met you once at Henri's and he talked about you like you were his son. And the only other time I ever talked to you was when you called to tell me he was in ICU." She started shaking.

"Maybe you should sit down. Can I get you something? A glass of water? A cup of tea? Maybe something stronger?"

Rainey plopped down on a couch that was covered by a floral bedspread. Her red glasses slipped and she pushed them back on her nose. "My heart's racing. Maybe a glass of wine would help. This is all so crazy. I'm scared. Really scared."

"I'll get it. The kitchen through there?"

"There should be some Chardonnay in the fridge. Oh my god, poor Alison. Poor Ji-min."

The kitchen was in the same shape as Rainey's hair. Jack opened the refrigerator and retrieved the only wine bottle. It had a yellow rubber stopper in it. He held it up to the light. It held less than a glass. He placed it on the counter and assumed the closed door at the rear of the kitchen led to a walk-in pantry. It did. Six-packs of diet cola filled one shelf. Boxes of pasta, brown rice, and lentils were on another. A plastic bucket held recyclables. Next to it was a cardboard wine case. The top had been opened and the four flaps folded closed. He undid them and pulled out a bottle. He could tell from the shape it wasn't a white. He glanced at the label. A 2001 Stag's Leap Cabernet Sauvignon. He slid it back in and pulled out another. It was a vintage Ridge Zinfandel. The third try got him a Chardonnay. He checked its label. A 2011 Pahlmeyer. He whistled silently. He checked a few more bottles. They were all high-end California labels. He closed the box without checking the rest and closed the pantry door. Back in the kitchen he emptied the bottle he'd left on the counter into a glass and poured himself a tumbler of water.

Rainey looked up from her phone when he returned. She placed it face down on her lap. Jack handed her the wine.

"You don't want any?" she asked.

He sat across from her. "I'm not big into wine and don't know much about it. You?"

She clutched the glass. "I get whatever's on sale at Trader Joe's but if someone else is buying..."

"Why did you call me?"

"I don't know. I guess I wanted somebody to talk to. Someone who knew Henri. I don't know that many people here. I hope you don't mind. I've never known anybody murdered before."

"It's okay to be scared so long as you don't give into panic."

"Thanks, I guess. What about Henri? Have you seen him? Has he come out of the coma yet?"

"Not yet. Everybody's pulling for him."

She took a gulp. Her hands shook. "Do you think what happened to Alison had anything to do with him?"

"I don't see how. He's an old man in a coma."

"I don't know why that policeman is making such a big deal about it."

"All cops can do is run down connections. Dolan found out she was a student nurse. He talked to the folks at the college. They told him about her classes and her job. He looked into that and saw you and Ji-min worked the same job. That's all. He's running down the connections."

"I suppose that makes sense." Her shoulders started to relax.

"Remind me, when did you start working for Henri?"

"Last fall at the beginning of the school year."

"And Alison and Ji-min?"

"Alison about the same time as me. Ji-min only started a few weeks ago. Maybe even less. Do you think... Do you think she's still alive?"

Jack glanced around the room. "You live alone?"

When Rainey said yes he said, "You have anybody who can come stay with you? A boyfriend or girlfriend? Family member?"

"They're all back east and I don't have a boyfriend at the moment. I mean, not really. Ugh." She clutched the wine glass. "I know that sounds pathetic. But I'm okay. I... well, there was this one guy. We went out for a while. He was really nice. Super successful. Super cute. Seemed super interested in me, what I was doing, you know, studying to be a nurse, working for Henri, doing rounds at Marin General. And then, he... Well, it's over now. It happens. It's hard. The city. Everybody into their own thing. Tech. Hedge funds. Making money. The whole online dating thing. Ugh. One day you're texting each other like a hundred times a day, going out to new restaurants, all the hip wine bars for special tastings, and then it's like you had it all wrong. Him all wrong." Her chin quivered. "Like I didn't mean a thing to him."

Rainey gulped the rest of her wine and then said wistfully, "I'll never read Charlotte Brontë again, that's for sure."

Jack put the glass of water down, eager to get out of there before the student nurse's fear and loneliness grew contagious. "What, *Wuthering Heights*?"

"No, that was written by Emily. Charlotte's the oldest sister, Anne was the youngest. Charlotte wrote *Villette*. It's one of my favorite novels. Was." She gazed into her empty wine glass and, as if speaking to it, quoted, 'He met her with caution, and replied to her in his softest tones, as if there was a kind of gossamer happiness hanging in the air which he feared to disturb by drawing too deep a breath.' "

12

Katie turned up Prince and danced to "Let's Go Crazy" as she cooked dinner. Chagall patrolled the kitchen. For an old dog his hearing and reflexes were still sharp. He could snag a grain of quinoa before it bounced twice. Lights shined at the ballpark but Jack knew they were only a tease. Opening day was still a couple of months off and roadies were readying the stadium for something else. A rock concert, maybe. A corporate bash, more likely. Tech start-ups always spent big on their launches. They weren't the first to stage a party to sell a product and grifters weren't the only ones who put on Prada to push a Ponzi.

"You seem pretty chipper," he said as he shredded parmesan. "Everything going good at the gyms?"

Katie did a quick 6-step and reverse as she sailed past, hip bumping him along the way. "I barely have to do anything. The staff is so empowered the gyms basically run themselves. All our classes are full, even trampoline trapeze. Our strategy of no dues and pay-what-you-can is a hit."

"You mean *your* strategy," he said.

"It's amazing what you can get done when you stop worrying about who gets the credit."

Katie slipped on a pair of oven mitts and opened the oven door. She pulled out two baking dishes and set them on ceramic trivets. Jack hummed the opening bars of "Ride of the Valkyries" before shifting to a Robert Duvall drawl: "I love the smell of lasagna in the morning."

"Don't worry. One's tofu and the other has meat for those of us still clinging to our Neanderthal ways."

Jack grunted. "Evolution not revolution. First Cro-Magnon, next filet mignon."

Katie's laugh prevented him from launching into a caveman rap complete with hand gestures. "Easy does it, Grog. Lug these to the table and I'll bring the wine. I think you're going to like it."

Chagall's nails clicked on the floor as he followed Jack. The loft was open with the exception of a wall separating the bedroom. Jack dimmed the lights so they would have a better view of the bay. Katie placed a glass of red wine next to his placemat before sitting down.

"This is nice," she said.

"What? The view or the meal?"

"All of it, the two of us having a quiet dinner alone."

Jack made a show of sniffing the air. "Not quite alone. There is Chagall."

"Seriously. I appreciate it all the more knowing how it's going to change. That makes it even more special, what we have now. You know what I mean?"

"All the books you've piled on my nightstand say a baby does sleep occasionally. Maybe we can sneak in a real meal together between the strained peas and pablum."

Another laugh confirmed the evening was shaping up fine. They ate for a while without need of further conversation. Jack sampled the wine. It was good. Better than good. It was very round, very full without being overbearing.

He held up the glass. "This must be a special meal for you to open a Brunello."

"You like it?"

"A lot. It's different. I can taste the earth. It's not from our stash in the closet, is it?"

She smiled mysteriously.

"Where's it from?" He named a couple of the more famous vineyards near the Tuscan town of Montalcino.

"It's not Italian," she said. "It's Californian."

"No way. Where did you find it?" He took another sip and was savoring it before swallowing.

"Grace gave it to me."

The mouthful came out in a spray.

THE WAY KATIE TOLD IT, she'd dropped by SF General on her way home from a gym she recently opened in the Bayview. While she was at Henri's bedside, a woman approached. Katie thought she was a doctor or a hospital administrator until she kissed Henri on the top of the head and patted his hand.

"You're Grace Millefiore, aren't you?" Katie said.

"I am. And you must be Jack's wife. He didn't tell me your name."

"It's Katie. And the fact that we're here at the same time is no accident, is it?"

"I see Jack's still attracted to intelligent women," Grace said.

Katie didn't take the bait. "Is this your first visit to see Henri?"

"I stop by every time I'm at the hospital." Grace stroked

Henri's hand. "Jack didn't tell you? My husband is a patient here but not for much longer. He's being discharged today."

"That must be a relief. If you don't mind me asking, what was wrong him?"

"The people who want to steal our water shot him."

Katie didn't flinch. "And that's why you called my husband for help."

"Does that bother you?"

"Only if he gets shot too."

"Jack used to be too fast to let anything like that happen."

"He still is."

Their eyes locked in a version of arm-wrestling as they assessed strengths and weaknesses. It was Katie who broke off first. She did so with a laugh. "Listen to us. We sound like we're in high school."

Grace's smile was slow to come. She brushed her hair back with her fingers. "It's going to be another hour before they finish my husband's paperwork. Would you like to go downstairs for a cup of coffee?"

"I'd love to."

The break in the rain cleared out the cafeteria some, and the women didn't have to step over any homeless people as they got their beverages and carried them to a table next to a window. No one was sleeping under it either.

Grace stirred her coffee and watched as Katie added honey to her herb tea. She started to say something but caught herself. Instead she asked, "Where did you and Jack meet?"

Katie told her about Nepal. "I was at a point in my life where I was frozen. It was like I was standing on top of Mount Everest and didn't know which way to turn. Jack took my hand and asked me to trust him. And so I did and..."

"Jumped and discovered you could fly."

"Crazy, isn't it?" She sipped her tea. "I'm not going to ask how you and Jack met or why you broke up. It's not because it would make me jealous. It's nothing like that at all. I don't want to take away from what you two had. Inserting myself into those memories would diminish them somehow. For both of you. Does that make sense?"

"You're not at all like I imagined," Grace said. "Jack's always been lucky. He still is. I can see that."

They shifted gears and finished their drinks while talking about their professions. Katie explained her business model for the gyms and outlined her prescription for women's health. Grace described how she and Stefan had to battle an aphid infestation that nearly destroyed their crop the first year.

"I've always liked the outdoors," Katie said. "When I was a little girl I imagined myself living on a ranch. It had horses and a big corral. Sometimes I wish I had a garden that's bigger than a few pots of herbs growing on the kitchen counter."

"You'll have to visit," Grace said. "You can work in our vineyard. We always need an extra pair of hands, especially during the harvest."

"I might take you up on that." Katie put her teacup down and stood. "This has been nice but I have to go."

"Are you parked in the garage? Good, I'll walk with you. I need to bring my car around front to pick up Stefan." Grace opened a compact and studied the mirror. "I have a case of wine in the car. I brought some as gifts for the hospital staff. I'd like to give you a bottle too. You can taste the fruits of our labor and hopefully it will convince you to come out to Clemens and pay us a visit. You do drink wine, don't you?"

Katie's palm went instinctively to her stomach. "I do but not right now."

Grace gave a final check in the compact's mirror before closing it. "Of course. How silly of me. Congratulations. Is this your first?"

13

The traffic signal in Clemens blinked yellow, and Jack slowed the Citroën as he approached the intersection. A semi hauling a single trailer approached from the right with its left-hand turn signal on so Jack braked and gave way. When the big rig completed its turn, he proceeded forward slowly. Another vehicle coming from the opposite direction had stopped too and was now making its way across. It was a pickup truck with a whip antennae and high suspension. Jack glanced at the driver. His complexion was orange and he wore a black ball cap with no logo. Tully sat next to him.

Jack started to pull a U-boat to follow them, but a red and yellow tongue licked the dusky sky, and a plume of embers and ash spiraled above it. He rolled the window down and smelled smoke close enough to taste. He floored the accelerator. The sedan went airborne as he crested the narrow bridge and flew over the canal. The road to Grace's came up fast and he yanked the hand brake as he cranked the wheel and took the turnoff in a Michelin-burning four-wheel drift. The tires all but screeched *Oh, merde!*

Jack released the brake and punched it. The road was oiled

gravel and not wide enough to warrant a center stripe. The speedometer was wavering on either side of eighty as he raced through an almond grove. The trees momentarily blocked his view of the flames. Once clear he could see the fire wasn't at Grace's but at a neighboring farm. No flashing red lights were in sight so he pulled into the drive and jumped out of the car.

Two men were training garden hoses on a burning barn. They might as well have been using squirt guns. People were shouting in Spanish. A little boy sat on the front stoop of a farmhouse clutching a singed chicken and wailed. Jack ran to the closest man holding a hose.

"Is anyone in there?" he shouted. "*Hay alguien en el granero? Son los animales?*"

"*Si,*" the man shouted back. "*Mi sobrino*. My nephew, Marco. He is trying to get the *caballos* out. Also a cow."

Jack grabbed the man's arm and directed the hose's spray on himself. Then he sprinted toward the barn. The words of his father screamed in his head: "First feel the door and then kiss the floor. Words to live by, *boyo*. Water will run while an axe'll get it done."

He spotted a stack of split firewood and a double-bladed axe stuck in a stump next to it. Jack grabbed the long hickory handle and wrenched it loose. He pulled his wet jacket over his head and entered the barn. The heat nearly knocked him flat. He crouched and looked around. One wall was ablaze. Pieces of burning straw swirled as if caught in a tornado. Over the roar of the flames and cracking timbers he could hear a cow bawling.

"Marco. Hey, Marco, where are you? *Adonde esta*?" he yelled twice.

"Over here." The voice was high and tiny, distorted by the sound-bending effect of the heat.

Jack ripped off the tail of his shirt and fashioned a mask. He kept his head hooded by the wet jacket and stayed as low as he could as he scrambled toward a row of stalls in the far corner. The first was open. A panicked cow pressed against the back wall stood over a trembling calf. Marco, a young man barely out of his teens, was trying to loop a rope around the cow's neck. Jack rushed in and threw his jacket over the animal's head. It quieted her long enough for Marco to fashion a halter.

"I'm going to lead her out," he said. "The calf will follow its mama."

"It's too young, too scared," Jack said. "The mama won't leave it behind. How 'bout we try it the other way around. I'll yank her and you grab the calf and carry it out. The mama should follow."

Marco wiped sweat beading on his face. He had the beginnings of a wispy moustache, and his goatee was more down than whiskers. "Okay, I give it a try."

Jack exchanged his grip on the axe for the rope and began tugging. The frightened cow dug in. He pulled harder. Marco kicked the cow's rear legs and she lurched forward. Then he snatched the calf and hoisted it on his shoulders.

"Go, go, go!" Jack shouted. "I'll lead the cow behind you."

"Okay but then I come back to save the horses. They're in the next stalls."

"Forget it. No time. The whole place is going up."

"I have to. It's my job."

Jack took the rope and tied it loosely around Marco's waist. "You take the cows. I'll free the horses. We'll be right behind you."

Marco staggered out with the calf. Jack yanked his jacket off the cow's head and spanked her. She fell in line and trotted right behind Marco.

Jack tried to ignore the deafening whoosh of wind that was buffeting the burning barn. The next stall had a wooden Dutch gate. The top half was open but the bottom was latched. A frenzied horse was inside kicking at the walls. Jack tried sliding the barrel bolt but it scorched his fingertips. He swung the axe. The jam splintered and the gate opened. The terrified horse reared, its eyes rolling white and front hooves punching the air. Jack flattened himself against the stall and inched his way to get beside the horse. Then he started waving his jacket and shouted the first thing that popped into his mind.

"Run, Seabiscuit! Run!"

The horse reared and then charged out of the stall. Jack didn't have time to see if it made it to safety. He ran to the next stall. The bottom half of the gate was closed. He hacked it open. A very fat mare was lying on the floor. Her enormous sides rose and fell like bellows as she struggled to breathe. Foam sprayed from her nostrils. Jack screamed at her, tugged on her mane, kicked her in the rump but she wouldn't budge.

The fire roared. Timbers crashed. Paint and chemicals exploded. Cans shot like missiles. Jack rushed out of the stall but flames raged. He retreated. A burning chunk of wood landed on the mare. He kicked it away but the mare's hide was on fire so he smothered the flames with his jacket. He felt tiny hoofs kicking from the inside.

"Come on, mama. Get up. Don't give in."

But it was no use. The mare was overcome by smoke. Jack hefted the double-bladed axe and swung.

One. Two. Three swings and the outside wall began to splinter. Four. Five. Six. A jagged hole big enough to see through opened and night air rushed in. It wouldn't take long for the voracious flames to detect a new source of fuel and come racing to gobble it up. Jack focused on the studs and thought of his father again and chopped as if felling trees.

Gavin McCoul was a son of a bitch through and through, a crook, a drunk, and abusive. Whenever he tried his hand at parenting, he did so in the form of a left to the jaw and a right to the gut. He'd hang out at the fire station during his off hours rather than go to one of his kids' birthday parties and spent more time at the United Irish Cultural Center hoisting boilermakers than he ever did going to mass at St. Joseph's. "You know why our kind's so good at fighting fires, *boyo*?" was a frequent rant. "It takes more than a bit o' luck o' the Irish. It takes big balls to knock down flames while laughing in their fookin' face."

Jack swung harder. He knocked out four studs and opened a hole the size of a horse. Then he dropped to his knees and wrenched the mare's head off the floor by grabbing her ears. He looked straight into her eyes and chomped down on her nose. It was soft and velvety and he bit so hard his teeth swam in blood. The mare whinnied and struggled to her feet. Jack slapped her ass and grabbed her tail and they galloped out into the night together as the roof came crashing down in a big red ball.

THE KID still clutched the chicken with burnt feathers and hadn't stopped crying. Jack sat beside him and watched the last flames flicker from the smoldering ruins of the barn. He felt as burned out as the fire, numbed after the man with the hose told him Marco had rushed back into the barn after bringing out the cow and calf.

"*Esta muerto*," he said, tears leaving streaks on his soot-covered face.

A fire truck finally showed up and a sheriff's patrol car was right behind. It was a case of better late than never not being nearly good enough. Not by a long shot. Deputy Santos got out of the patrol car and walked quickly to the farmer and his wife. They hugged and spoke for a few minutes. When the farmer pointed toward him she came over.

"What are you doing here?" she demanded.

Jack held a jug of water. He pointed it at the heap of embers. "What you said about this community? Clearly not everyone got the part about being neighborly."

Deputy Santos's head cocked. A short ponytail hung below the broad brim of her hat. "What's that supposed to mean?"

"This was no accident. You need to call for an arson investigation." Jack gulped some more water. "And while you're at it, call for a homicide team. The kid who died here, Marco? It was murder."

She adjusted her duty belt. A holstered semiautomatic, ammo clips, and a flashlight hung from it. "What makes you say that?"

The firetruck's spots and headlights were directed at the barn. Firefighters sprayed water on the dying embers.

Jack stood. "Do you know if the farmer owns or rents?"

"What does that have to do with anything?"

"Plenty. Do you know or not?"

The deputy hesitated. "I do. He's my uncle."

Jack blew out air. "I apologize. Was Marco your brother?"

"A cousin."

"I'm sorry for your loss."

"My uncle owns this farm. It's been in the family for a hundred years."

"The water rights too?"

"Of course. Why do you ask?"

"Because I think whoever started the fire wanted to send a message. And if I'm right, it's all about the water, especially allotments that are old and worth a lot. Can we talk to your uncle?"

"You're not in law enforcement, are you?"

"No."

"That's what I thought. I can't have you interfering." She crossed her arms.

Jack gulped more water. "Come on, deputy. You said it yourself. Few things out here are like they are in the big city. But if I'm right, this fire is from the big city. Guess what? So am I. Let's help each other out."

Deputy Santos thought about it before leading Jack across the yard. Her uncle's name was Manny. He called her Florencia. He said to Jack, "Thank you for what you did. The mare is my wife's favorite. She's going to name the foal after you."

Jack bowed to the aunt. "I'd be honored if you named it after Marco instead."

That triggered a round of tears. Afterward, the deputy asked Manny if anyone had approached him about his water rights.

"Some men come and ask to buy them. But it makes no sense. How can I farm without water?"

"What were their names?"

"They did not say."

"Can you describe them?"

"*Gringos*. White men."

Jack said, "How did they react when you said no?"

"They offered more money. They offered to buy my land. But I said no. A thousand times no. Sell my land? It is not mine to sell. It is my father's, my grandfather's. It is my children's. My grandchildren's."

Deputy Santos put her hand on her uncle's shoulder. "*No se preocupe, tio.* No one is going to take your land." She gestured to Jack, and they stepped away. "This has something to do with what happened at the Fabros, doesn't it?"

"I think so."

"What are the Fabros to you, family?"

"No."

"Did they hire you? Are you a private detective?"

He said no with a shake of his head as he gulped more water.

"Then tell me who's behind it?"

"I have some ideas, that's all."

The brim of her hat couldn't mask her frustration. "I insist. And that's an order. I can arrest you if you don't."

"All I have is a couple of hunches. Proof is something altogether different. I'm going to keep looking. Given what's been going on, it shouldn't be too hard to find something. When I do I'll let you know."

"I can't let you do that. This is a police matter. If you're right about the fire here, then it's a capital crime."

"And who would be in charge of the investigation? You?"

Santos adjusted her duty belt again. "Our substation covers two hundred square miles. We don't have the resources. I'll do what I did with the Fabro shooting. I'll turn it over to the major crimes investigation unit from Stockton. That's protocol."

"You heard anything back from them? Anybody come out and take a look around, canvas the neighborhood?"

She hesitated. "Their priority is meth and the gangs."

Jack shifted his weight. His quads ached. "All the more reason we need to look into this quietly and not stir something up before the department is ready to deal with it."

"We?"

"Yeah, we. You and me. For Marco."

"And how do you propose *we* go about it?"

"How about if you talk to the fire crew and let them know you think this could be an arson. They'll have to put it in their report and that will trigger an investigation. It could smoke out who's behind this. I'll dig around on my end and see what I can find out about people trying to corner the water market."

Santos didn't say yes but she didn't say no either. Instead she asked him what he was going to do next.

"That's easy," Jack said. "Head over to the Fabros and ask if I can take a shower before sitting down to dinner."

14

————

Stefan was gritting his teeth at the dinner table. Earlier he'd found Jack half naked and holding his wife. It all started when Jack was drying off after taking a shower. Grace gave a quick knock on the guest bathroom door and entered. She was carrying a set of Stefan's clothes.

"I brought you these." She watched as Jack knotted a towel around his waist.

"Thanks," he said. "I may have run your well dry scrubbing the soot off."

Grace wore an artisan silver necklace and matching earrings that caught the bathroom's light and made her black hair seem even glossier. She brushed droplets of water from the shamrock tattoo on Jack's shoulder.

"Remember when I got a little one like it to surprise you? Took you a while to find it."

"Couldn't forget, don't you know?"

Her fingertips stayed on his arm. "I told Stefan about us. He had the right to know, the same as Katie. She told me when we met at the hospital."

"You shouldn't have set her up like that."

Grace's hand fell to her side. "I didn't set anybody up. Did I think I might run into her? I hoped I would."

"I'm not going to say it twice. I agreed to help you but Katie stays out of it. That's the deal."

"Of course," she said softly. "I was going to tell you how much I like her and how happy I am for you. I'm glad you found each other. Whatever you may think, I really did care how things turned out for you. I've always wanted the best for you."

"Right."

"I think you'll make a wonderful father too."

"That's a switch." As soon as he said it he knew how it sounded.

Her lips formed an *o* but no words came out. She dropped the clothes and left.

Jack didn't waste any time going after her. He caught up to her in the hallway and grabbed her by the arm and spun her around. "Wait. That's not what I meant."

"Yes, it was." Her voice wavered.

"I meant you've changed from always looking for the angles. That is a switch. A big switch. I didn't mean the other thing."

"The other thing?"

"You know what I mean."

"Careful, Jack. You're starting to sound like you care what I think."

He kept his mouth shut. He didn't know if he was seeing the real her or who she wanted him to see.

Stefan shuffled down the hall. He halted and leaned on a cane. His stare traveled from the towel to Jack's bare chest to his hand clutching his wife's arm. "Am I interrupting something?"

Grace volleyed his sarcasm. "Don't worry, dear. Jack and I were reminding each other why we're married to other people."

She slipped away and when she was gone, Stefan hobbled

closer. He raised the crook of his cane to Jack's face. "My clothes better be the only thing you're borrowing around here."

The mood remained strained as they finished dinner. Jack told them about the fire next door.

Stefan said, "What makes you so sure it was lit by the same group that chucked a bottle of gas at our cellar? Barns catch fire all the time. They're full of fertilizer and pesticides. It could've been a spark from a trash fire."

"I talked to the farmer. He said some people were trying to buy his water rights."

"Do you know how often I get calls from farmers and brokers and representatives from other irrigation districts looking to buy my allotments? Speculators are as plentiful as spam."

Grace caught Jack's glance and said, "Jack's been looking into Jonathan Gossamer and the bodyguard he travels with. He saw him driving through Clemens right after the fire started."

Stefan twirled his linguine. "So what? It doesn't change anything. We're not going to hand over our water and we're not going to let anybody run us off. I told McCoul that when he barged into my hospital room."

Jack knew it was pointless arguing with him. Pride and naiveté were a lethal combination. "If you're not going to give up your water, then the only choice is to stop Gossamer and his crew. Maybe we can find enough to tie him to the fire next door and have him arrested."

"If he's as slick as you say he is, how likely is the sheriff's department going to find any evidence?"

"There's two sides to slick," Jack said. "He'll slip and fall if someone pushes him."

"And who would that be, you?" Stefan threw his napkin down on the table.

Grace said. "I'm sure Jack will think of something."

Her tone mixed challenge with temptation. Jack could hear all the conversations they'd ever had, the plans they discussed when finding a mark, weighing the pros and cons of the type of play they'd pull, writing the scripts, and practicing the lines and moves over and over again until they had their roles down pat. Most of all he remembered how they celebrated after a big score. One time they didn't leave a hotel suite for three days and nights.

He picked up his wine glass, smelled it, breathed it in, and then closed his eyes and took a sip. He couldn't tell if he was tasting the oak from the aging barrel or the wood from the burning barn just as he couldn't tell if Grace had been planning something all along.

Noise from a powerful engine filled the silence. Gravel crunched under tires. The roar of a second engine followed.

Jack looked out the window. "Two pickup trucks are in the drive. I can't tell how many people. They've got their headlights on as well as off-road light bars on the roofs."

The trucks came to a stop side-by-side. The drivers left their lights on and engines running.

Stefan started to get up. "I've got a shotgun and a hunting rifle. I hope you know how to shoot."

"Nobody's shooting anybody. You two sit tight. I'll got out and see what's what. Understood?"

"Jack," Grace said.

"Stay here." He palmed a steak knife and slid it into his back pocket before opening the front door. As he stepped onto the porch, he avoided looking directly at the headlights.

"Can I help you?" he called.

The only answer was the rumble of the trucks' engines. He raised his hand and mimed rolling down a window.

"I can't hear you. Can I help you?"

Again, no response.

There were at least two people to deal with but no way of knowing if others were hiding in the beds. If they'd come to storm the castle, a piece of cutlery in his pocket wasn't going to stop them.

A third pair of headlights turned up the drive. They were too low to the ground to be a truck's. Jack kept both hands visible and started down the steps. That's when the shotgun boomed. He ducked instinctively as a flight of birdshot zinged overhead.

"What the hell?" shouted the driver of the closest truck. He scrambled from the cab and used the door as a shield. He held a black semiautomatic gangsta style.

"Hold it!" Jack yelled. "Calm down. Everybody calm down."

The driver of the second truck started shouting. "Eddie, you hit? You want me to take 'em? Talk to me, Eddie. You hit?"

Jack kept his hands up. "Calm. Calm. Calm," he said like one of Katie's mantras.

Stefan Fabro sprawled on the porch, knocked over by the recoil from a 12-gauge shotgun. He'd bit his lip and it was bleeding. The fall tore the stitches in his chest and twin red bouquets bloomed on his shirt too.

Grace rushed out. "Jack, do something."

"He'll be okay. He's not shot."

The third vehicle pulled up behind the two trucks. The driver got out and ambled over.

"So, *ese*," Hark said. "This the way they welcome homies here in the boonies?"

15

Eddie and Chaco were brothers. Hark got the pair settled in the guesthouse next to the wine cellar before joining Jack on the front porch.

"I could get used to country living," he said as he sat on the porch swing. "Fresh air, no traffic, no nothing. I say we leave the trucks right where they're at. Sends a message to anyone drives up."

"The gun racks hanging in the back windows being the exclamation points. Those and the red and black Norteños stickers," Jack said.

"Hey, you asked for dudes who could carry their weight. So they got their experience on the streets. Lots of people did."

"I do appreciate their professionalism when Fabro let loose with the shotty. Of course a little advance warning you were showing up tonight could've saved on some bandages."

"I did call. Sent a text too. You never got back. I figured you had your hands full." He hooked a thumb at Grace's front door and grinned.

"That's right, my phone. It's all but melted in my jeans." He gave a quick recap.

"*Chingame*," Hark said. "That's a helluva way to go. I saw it a few times back in the sandbox. Artillery hitting mud houses. Dudes stepping on a IED. You sure it was Tully you saw?"

"No doubt about it. He was traveling with another man who's probably ex-military too. Had a complexion like a navel orange. We'll need to find out who he is."

"The third little pig. Chances are they served together. Easy enough to run down." Hark set the porch swing swinging. "What about the local Five-O? Aren't they doing anything?"

"I've only met a deputy but she seems on the up-and-up. It was her uncle's place they burned. Marco is her cousin."

"You tell her about Goss and Tully?"

"I held back for now. She doesn't have the resources to deal with guys like them."

"If you think Eddie and Chaco aren't enough horsepower I can get more."

"If it comes to it. Better if it doesn't turn into a shooting match."

"Okay. So we go at it another way. You come up with a plan to take them down?"

"Something tells me Grace already has."

Hark stopped the swing. "She has, huh? This plan of hers, you sure it won't take us down with it?"

"Only one way to find out."

JACK FOUND Grace sitting in front of a computer. Bookshelves lined one wall of the room. A four-drawer file cabinet stood opposite. Framed watercolors hung on either side. One was of a ranch with a cluster of low, red-tile roof buildings in the middle and steep mountains in the background. The other was an open air market scene with women wearing bowler hats and wrapped in bright blankets sitting behind baskets filled with fresh fruits and vegetables.

"How's the patient?" Jack asked.

"Stefan was in a lot of pain so I doubled his meds. He'll be asleep until morning."

"He took quite a bump."

"You must think him a fool but he's never had to deal with something like this. Stefan's a good man."

"We both know good can still get you killed. Worse, it can get others killed. Eddie and Chaco can't do their job if Stefan doesn't let them. Okay?"

"I'll talk to him." Grace paused. "Where's Hark?"

"He went home. He's going to find out who Gossamer's other hired gun is."

"I'm surprised he agreed to help. Hark's never liked me."

"Maybe not but you can trust him with your life. He's the only man I know who doesn't think about himself first. It's the way he's wired."

Jack went on to explain how Hark never had a father to speak of and his mother had to leave him with his *abuela* to go find work in LA. She never came back. When he was growing up on the rough and tumble streets in the Mission, Hark always looked out for his grandma and friends, whether they were a classmate at Saint Joe's or a member of his gang. He always put it on the line for them. He did the same thing when he went to Afghanistan.

"You mean his personal code. Honor and all that." Grace pushed her hair back. "You're the same way."

"Katie says we're more like an old married couple than brothers, knowing what each other thinks, knowing what the other's going to do before he does it."

"I'm surprised she's been able to get between you two. I never could."

"Katie doesn't want to. She knows she doesn't have to worry about me as long as Hark's around."

Sadness darkened Grace's blue eyes. "I never had a sister. Someone I could talk to, share secrets with. Someone I could trust."

"But now you got Stefan and the winery." He took a breath. "Look, I know you've thought of some way to protect what you got, and it doesn't matter to me if it was part of a play you were hatching all along. Gossamer and Tully got to go down no matter what. They can't get away with murdering Marco and terrorizing who knows how many others. I think they're linked to another killing too."

"Another farmer?"

"Someone in the city. I'm not positive but..." He let it drop and walked over to the paintings. "Are these of Argentina?"

"The one of the *estancia* is. The other is Bolivia. Stefan and I took a holiday there. It has some of the oldest vineyards in the New World."

"Did you consider buying property there when you were looking?"

"Not really. The wine market is localized and there's not much in the way of distribution channels. All we bought was that painting and some jewelry. Bolivia has some of the oldest silver mines in the world too." She touched her silver necklace as she spoke.

Jack studied the paintings some more. "What are you working on?"

Grace clicked a few keys. A map of California popped open. "What's the first thing Henri taught us?"

"You can't cheat an honest man."

"That too but more importantly it was the only thing more blinding than greed is ego. Even when a mark suspects he's being conned, he'll convince himself he can beat you at your own game. Whatever the payoff is supposed to be, he'll always want something bigger." She smiled. "Remember the blue pearl?"

"How could I forget."

The blue pearl was a long con they pulled on a jewel fence. Jack and Grace learned he was holding a sizeable stash of hot rocks. They posed as cat burglars trying to sell a legendary diamond named the blue pearl because of its unusual shape, size, and color. The backstory was it had been heisted years before and never seen again. Jack and Grace said they'd come across it by happenstance when ripping off a private collector. The fence saw through their scam, as they'd planned he would and proposed a partnership where they would pull the same swindle on a new rival who was undercutting his prices. Jack and Grace maneuvered their mark into adding his stash of stolen diamonds to help sell the fake blue pearl to the rival. The fence didn't discover until too late that the rival was part of the grift and played by Henri LeConte. The trio made off with all the real diamonds and the fence wound up with the fake along with some very angry clients who demanded payment for the stones he'd lost.

"We made a good team," Grace said.

Jack didn't disagree. "What's your idea for a blue pearl here, tow an iceberg down from the North Pole?"

"I'm still working it out." Grace tapped the digitalized map and it zoomed in on the Central Valley. She tapped it again to reveal an overlying screen of colored squares and connecting lines like those on a subway map. "The squares represent reservoirs and the lines represent canals and aqueducts. The reservoirs store thirteen million acre feet of water. The canal system transports more than half that amount every year."

"How big is an acre foot?"

"Two would fill an Olympic size swimming pool."

Jack leaned over to get a closer look. "What are these dotted lines?"

"The boundaries of irrigation districts. They're self-governing cooperatives. They levy taxes and borrow money to pay for water and then allocate it to their members."

"And if you're a member with senior water rights that makes you the big fish in the pond."

"Now you can see why Gossamer is going after them in particular. I don't think he's trying to corner the market so much as he's trying to make it look like he has a bunch of senior rights already that he can package and sell to investors he'll later wind up leaving high and dry. We need to figure out a way to offer him something bigger than picking off one senior rights holder at a time."

Jack picked up the makings of a play. It felt like old times. "We get him to think he can snag a bunch in one fell swoop and then pull the rug out from under him."

"What if created a big store of some kind, an entity that represents senior rights holders? He'll convince himself he can outmaneuver it and wind up with the lot."

"One-stop shopping." Jack stroked his jaw. "The problem is it would come with lots of holes that need plugging and requires lots of players. If the goal is to get him busted rather than make a score, there won't be anything to pay off a large crew. There's another hitch. Gossamer has been at this for a while so he'd know if such an outfit existed."

Jack focused on the map. He traced hash marks that outlined an oblong swath. "What do these boundaries represent? They're not county lines."

"They mark out groundwater basins. There are hundreds in California. Look at this map overlay." Grace clicked keys and the screen showed a jigsaw puzzle of the state with all the pieces shaded in different colors. "Most are fed by underground streams and seeps from lakes. Some are filled mechanically."

"How come?"

"Underground storage has less evaporation compared to a surface reservoir. They call it water banking."

Jack tapped the screen. "You mean they're the equivalent of vaults filled with liquid gold. You seem to know a lot about this."

"I have to. No water, no wine."

Jack weighed her reply. "So what happens to all this underground water?"

"If a basin is below a farmer's land and easily reached by a well, the water is used right there for irrigation. When a basin is really big, the excess water is put into the aqueduct system and sold on the open market."

Jack tapped the screen again. "I think one of these could be our blue pearl."

"You could be on to something." Grace typed and the map of the Central Valley zoomed. "I told you Stefan's great-grandfather once owned most of the county."

"You also said all that was left is the patch you're living on."

"What I meant was our vineyard is the best of the lot for growing grapes. Not all of the Fabro land was sold because some of it was considered worthless. See this huge chunk here? It's called Sabbia Plain. It's really a sink. Most of it is covered by a shallow alkali lake that's dry most of the year. The surface is the color and consistency of baking soda."

"Could there be a groundwater basin under it?"

"It all depends on the soil underneath." She clicked the keyboard and another overlay appeared. "These lines represent elevation contours. Sabbia Plain is boxed in by the flanks of the mountains. Water runs downhill. With the right soils, the water would collect underground in a high runoff year. But any water that did would quickly become contaminated by all the alkali. That's why Sabbia Plain has never been farmed or wells put in."

"Doesn't matter. All we have to do is make it look like it's full of good water thanks to El Niño. A few drilling reports, a couple of geological studies left in the right place could do that."

"Do you know someone who can create those?"

"I do. But remember, we're talking about pulling a blue pearl. We'll need to leave the window open a crack so Gossamer can spot it as a fake when we play it on him. A guy like him? Id will beat ego every time. When he finds out we're trying to scam him, he'll want it all the more to prove he can beat us and run the play himself."

Grace's expression hardened. "We'll need to make the trap strong enough so he can't wiggle free when it springs. He'll be even more dangerous if he gets out. We can't let that happen."

"Goes without saying," Jack said but he wondered if anything could be built strong enough to hold Tully too.

16

Katie was breathless when she answered the phone as if she were in the gym doing Zumba or working out on the speed bag.

"Guess what? Henri regained consciousness. It was only for a few seconds but the doctor says it's a very good sign. Henri's going to pull through. I'm sure of it."

Jack's first response was to ask if he said anything.

"He couldn't because he's still on the ventilator. But he opened his eyes and smiled at me. You know that smile of his? Like he's in on a big secret."

Jack stood in Grace's kitchen looking out the window. The vineyards were dark. Starlight was scattered between clouds like a shotgun blast. He thought of Henri's photos and wondered if he was finally going to learn what secrets they held.

"Did the doctor say how long it will take him to recover? Will he be able to remember things and talk?"

"They're going to run some tests. Taylor told me she's going to work every shift so she'll be there when Henri wakes up again." Katie caught her breath. "You're not calling from your cell. Where are you?"

"I'm still at Grace's. It's been a long day." He gave her a sanitized version of the fire next door.

"But you're okay? You didn't get burned?"

"Only my phone did. I called to let you know I'm going to be late."

"Okay but before I forget, Terry called. He's been trying to reach you. I guess he doesn't know about your phone."

Jack knew the homicide detective still kept Katie's number on his favorites. "What did he want?"

"He told me to tell you it was important and to call him right away. He said it's about a nurse."

"Did he mention a name?"

"Rainey. Like the weather."

IT WAS midnight by the time Jack rolled into Golden Gate Park. He parked in front of a two-story stucco building next to Kezar Stadium, the long-ago home of the 49ers. Trees rustled in the wind and creatures rustled in the bushes. Some were two-legged. Fresh graffiti marred a corner of SFPD's Park Station. The writer must have been new in town or jacked on meth to tag the cops.

Jack's entry into the waiting room was captured on a CCTV screen. A gruff voice barked over an intercom. "Help you?"

"Name's McCoul. Lieutenant Dolan asked me to meet him here."

"Empty your pockets and stick it all in the can and slide it through the slot."

Jack did as he was ordered. A reinforced door swung open. An overweight desk sergeant with a salt and pepper natural directed him upstairs. Terry was in the situation room. Jack figured he'd picked Park Station because it was central to the three nurses' apartments. Photographs and timelines were pinned to a corkboard. Stacks of papers and paper coffee cups crowded a long folding table, the kind schools and churches use for potlucks. The homicide cop's navy blue suit jacket hung on the back of a chair. The sleeves of his white shirt were rolled up and his rep tie loosened.

"What were you doing out in the valley?" he asked.

Jack already guessed Katie would've told him where he was at. What he didn't know was how much Terry knew about Grace.

"Visiting an old friend. Katie said you wanted to talk about Rainey. What happened?"

Her photograph was taped to a whiteboard between two headshots that were blowups of school ID cards. Names were printed below them in dry erase marker.

"You want to tell me why your fingerprints are all over her apartment?"

"She called, I went. She was pretty shook up after you got through interrogating her."

"Nobody interrogated anybody. She was interviewed."

"Call it what you want but you didn't offer her police protection either. She's scared out of her mind. What's her picture doing on the board?"

"I'm the one asking questions here. When was the last time you saw her?"

He told him.

"You must know her pretty well to be the one she reaches out to after her friend was murdered."

"I thought you said you were the one asking questions."

Terry flashed annoyance. "Why you?"

"Because of Henri. I told her about his heart attack. I'd met her once before at his place. It was a while back. Is she dead or alive?"

"She's at SF General on a seventy-two hour suicide hold. A

beat cop picked her up flying down the middle of Haight Street. She was loaded with enough Schedule Fours to tranquilize one of the buffaloes they keep here in the park. My guess is we'll find out she stole them from work."

"They're bison. They call it the Buffalo Paddock but the animals are American bison. The song's got it wrong. Buffaloes only roam in Africa and Asia."

"You think that's funny? Nothing about this is funny. I got one murdered nurse, another who tried to kill herself, and a third who vanished. Somehow they're all connected to you."

"I told you, Rainey was rattled by Alison's death. I asked her if she had anyone she could stay with but she said all her family's back east."

"Rhode Island."

"Okay, Rhode Island."

"What else did you two talk about?"

"That's about it. I wasn't there very long."

"That was it? You talked and then left?"

Jack's radar pinged. "She asked for a glass of wine so I got it for her. A few minutes later I was out of there."

"How many glasses did she drink?"

"Only the one that I know of."

"You didn't have any?"

"A little early in the day, don't you know?"

Terry's lips tightened. He was a tea-totaler, a legacy of growing up with an old-school beat cop for a father who spent as much time at the United Irish Cultural Center as Jack's dad.

"Then how come your prints are on a case of wine in the closet? Answer me that."

The homicide cop had been on the job too long to allow a look of triumph cross his face, but there was a hint of it in his voice.

Jack repeated the steps as if he was reading the instructions for assembling Swedish furniture. "Rainey asked for a glass of wine. I went to the fridge. The bottle was nearly empty. I looked around for a full one. I checked the pantry. I saw the box. I searched for a bottle of white. The ones I found were pretty high-end so I figured she was saving them for a special occasion." He looked at the board with the photos. Dates and times were listed in a column. "I'm surprised a judge issued you a search warrant to fingerprint her apartment. Since when is attempted suicide a crime?"

He let it hang but Terry wasn't about to touch it. "That's some pretty expensive wine for a student nurse."

"You tell me."

"I just did."

"What did you do, run down to BevMo and check on prices?"

"Katie told me you were out in the valley visiting Grace Millefiore."

Jack didn't blink at the changeup.

Terry hurled another. "And Grace is now married to Stefan Fabro. The Fabros are to wine what the Irvines are to real estate."

Jack kept quiet.

"Grace Millefiore. I've been doing some checking. She was in the system. Her juvenile records are locked but there were plenty of accusations lodged against her as an adult. She disappeared for a few years and now she turns up as an in-law to one of California's oldest families. Quite a step up. Or should I say *setup*? I hear you two were quite the pair. Or should I say *are*?"

"Were, Terry, were. It's all past tense. That's how it is when a relationship's over. Try and remember that."

The cop's jaw twitched. "What I don't know is why Rainey has the same box of expensive wine in her closet like her dead friend Alison."

"Maybe they went in together to get a discount."

"Maybe. But I wonder what we'd find if we took a trip out to your past tense girlfriend's and looked in her closet?"

17

S outh Park was a secret garden in the heart of San Francisco, a block long green oval crowded with benches and playground equipment and surrounded by trees. The flats and low brick buildings that ringed the bucolic patch formed a tiny enclave within the sprawling South of Market neighborhood.

At the corner of South Park Street and Jack London Alley stood a former tool and die shop. Its exterior sported an alligator paint job complete with a front door that resembled a gaping, toothy maw. Grade school letters printed on a chalkboard spelled out the tenant's name: Parish Cybersecurity. Computer workstations filled the ground floor and their operators were either keyboarding standing up or sitting on Pilates balls. Headsets, T-shirts, and jeans were the uniform of choice and beards and nose rings de rigueur. Jack counted three dogs and a flat-faced cat wearing a studded black leather collar.

The company's founder perched on the edge of a stool in the middle of the scrum. Candy apple red Beats gleamed atop his shaved head as he orchestrated a giant keyboard connected to three screens like a DJ at the hottest club in town. DuPree Davis was basketball player tall and lean, but with none of the tattoos. He went by the handle Do Pray, and when he spotted Jack he shouted a *hey*.

"You're a sight for sore eyes. I apologize if I haven't been round to see y'all. There's days I never get outa here we so busy."

"Can't say I'm surprised how your enterprise has taken off. You were bound for tech glory the moment you stepped off the Dog from Louisiana."

The young man pushed back the Beats but hip-hop still poured from them. "Thanks to you giving me a job and then selling your start-up and paying me for the work I done."

"Plenty of times I regret selling but as the saying goes, I got an offer I couldn't refuse." Jack glanced around the crowded room. "Is there a place we can talk in private? I may have another job for you."

"We got a nap room upstairs. Long as no one's using it, we can visit a spell."

Jack followed the lanky programmer past a Ping-Pong table to a twilit room with rubber yoga mats on the floor. Radio Sri Chinmoy played softly through Bluetooth speakers.

"I can turn that off if you want," Do Pray said. "Those tracks aren't my style but people like it calm when they come in to recharge. They working awful hard."

"Katie plays the same thing when she's doing yoga. Look, what I wanted to ask was something that may not exactly fit in with your new business model. Feel free to say no."

"Why would I do that?"

"I heard you're working for some pretty mainline companies now."

"We got a few that come calling, that's for sure. Insurance, software, even universities. Everybody's got to protect their data."

"You're daylighting backdoors and throwing up walls and moats to keep the hackers out?"

"That's part of it. There's more. What y'all need?"

"I don't need to hack information from a system. I need to hack some in. And I need to make it easy to find when people go looking for it."

Do Pray rubbed his chin. "You're trying to help someone out again like last time. I can get behind that. What's it all about?"

"Best if I only give you the bare bones. A friend of mine is being threatened by some pretty nasty people. We came up with a way we think will stop them."

"That's good 'nough for me. How can I help?"

"I need to get into the California Department of Water Resources database and change some hydrogeological maps and well drilling records already in there so they say what I want them to say and put in a deed that shows a recent change of ownership."

"Sounds easy 'nough. We been doing work for a couple of government agencies now. They don't spend much on security, so anybody with a smart phone can get in. What you need the maps and records to show?"

"I have a list but it all boils down to the most recent ones showing the property now has a lake the size of Tahoe beneath it because of El Niño. Now here's the wrinkle. I need it all to look legit but there has to be one little mistake a pro will catch so he knows it's been faked."

The meditation music had switched tracks. Now the instruments had given way to chanting. Jack could see Katie doing downward dog, her growing belly straining against her tank and crops as he waited for Do Pray to respond.

The programmer was bobbing to a different kind of music as he thought. "Got it. We add a second author in the properties box. People always forget to edit that when they changing an original document. Real simple like. Okay. No problem. When you need it done by?"

"Sooner the better. The bad guys are short on patience."

"Give me the list and I'll get on it. I'll also put in a tracker so when these folks find it it'll let you know."

"You sure you're all right with this?"

"Fo' sure. I owe you big time."

"Okay but promise me this. The ones who will come looking are dangerous. Don't leave anything that can lead back to you. And if it looks like it's going south, pull the plug and we'll figure out another way. Deal?"

Do Pray did what he used to do back home in Terrebonne Parish. He spit on his palm before shaking.

CICERO BROADSHANK, Esq. was slurping oysters at Waterbar. A plate heaped with fried calamari and another with a dozen jumbo shrimp fashioned like a crown around a bowl of Louis dressing joined the platter of iced Kumamotos on the half shell.

"Jack, my boy!" San Francisco's most famous criminal defense lawyer bellowed. "Take a seat. I took the liberty of ordering us both abalone steaks. The chef assures me they were clinging to a rock in sixty feet of water off Mendocino not three hours ago."

Broadshank was commanding his usual booth with its sweeping view of the Embarcadero and bay beyond. Jack kept the table between them. He knew better than to sit beside him. The corpulent counselor approached dining with the same gusto as a hockey player body checking an opponent against the boards. A bottle of Pinot Grigio peeked from a silver ice bucket. A waiter scurried over and filled Jack's glass. Broadshank picked up a shrimp that was as plump and pink as his thumb.

"As always I must remind you that everything we discuss here is attorney-client privileged and anything said or described is purely hypothetical." He chomped the shrimp in half. "Try one. They're boiled in champagne and then lightly grilled in olive oil more virgin than anybody in this town. Your retainer is up to date, is it not my boy?"

Jack passed on the shrimp but tried an oyster. It was sweet and tangy all in one swallow. He picked up another. "Remember Grace Millefiori?"

"How could I forgot her? So beautiful and such an interesting client. Where is she these days? I have not heard from her since you two left on a European tour. When was that? Three, four years ago?"

"She lives on a vineyard near Clemens."

"You don't say? And what is she doing there?"

"What people who live on vineyards do."

"Grace is a winemaker? Imagine that. A true metamorphous. She always was a butterfly. Good for her. What is the winery? I probably know it." His picked up his wineglass. It disappeared in a meaty paw as he drained it.

"San Stefan. Named after her husband. Stefan Fabro."

Broadshank sat up straighter. He smoothed the linen napkin he'd tucked into the neck of his custom-made shirt. He always wore black suits with wide chalk lines and a matching yellow silk tie and pocket hankie. They were as memorable to juries as his mane of white hair and theatrical baritone.

"Grace wed a Fabro? You don't say. Now that is a family of high social standing."

Jack knew the lawyer really meant high net worth. "You ever do any work for them?"

"Jack, my boy. You know I only specialize in defending clients who have been unjustly accused by a law enforcement structure in dire need of reform. Dare I say a complete overhaul from top to bottom. Police malfeasance is one matter, a corrupt court system another." His shudder made his copious jowls flap. "I am certain the Fabro family retains a white shoe firm to manage their myriad legal affairs." He speared a forkful of calamari and chewed thoughtfully. "But if a family member were to be implicated in a criminal matter, surely inadvertently of course, I would be honored to make myself available for consultation."

Jack sipped some Pinot Grigio. It was cold and crisp with a hint of pear. "Would that include counsel on how to use or even circumvent certain codes and statutes in order to protect their assets? Hypothetically speaking, of course."

Broadshank eyed the three platters of seafood arranged in front of him, but Jack was sure he was seeing bounty of a different nature all together. He tut-tutted. "That would depend on a number of factors but suffice to say, case law is filled with precedential extenuating circumstances that can be proffered to justify certain actions and thus not breach legality."

The waiter ferried over two plates. The abalone had been pounded to perfection, breaded very lightly, and cooked in a shallot, garlic, and wine reduction. Broadshank took a bite. "Exquisite. My compliments to the chef."

As soon as the waiter disappeared, the defense attorney said, "So my boy, you have my curiosity. Tell me more about this suppositional situation our fictional friends might find themselves in and do share the theoretical solution they may or may not be contemplating."

Jack looked down at his plate to cover his smile. Abalone were gastropods and that made them snails, pure and simple. But no restaurant, and certainly not one with an enviable Zagat rating, ever referred to them as such. They were billed as shellfish, the same as lobsters were, even though they were anthropods whose members include cockroaches and black widows.

"Let me tell you a story that's as old as the hills. It's about a family of pioneers." Jack took a bite of abalone. "The family worked hard and over time became rich in land and water. But then a gang of outlaws threatened to steal all they had. The family asked the local constabulary for help but the outlaws had superior numbers."

Broadshank shook his fork. "I must advise you to cease and desist. I have heard this story before. A mysterious stranger rides into town and guns down all the bandits before riding off into the sunset with the rancher's wife. It is not a tale I wish to be a party to, not even hypothetically. Never, I repeat never, would I ever condone such a course of events nor be associated with it, no matter how remotely." He belched loudly.

"Hear me out, CB. This is a different story because they use land not lead to beat the bad guys. And guess what? The real hero is a lawyer who saves the day by providing counsel on a legal strategy that will become the stuff of legends. They'll be talking about it at California Bar meetings for years to come."

Cicero Broadshank cocked his head. After a few minutes he turned his attention back to the main course. "This abalone is to my liking. Go on, my boy, continue your tale."

18

H enri LeConte was a bantamweight who never let size
get in the way of his big dreams and even bigger
cons. Some people swore he was Parisian-born,
schooled at Ecole de Beaux-Arts, and directed art restoration at
the Louvre. Others claimed he was an autistic savant who'd been
raised by Gypsies and painted ceilings in great cathedrals. A few
were convinced he was the bastard son of Henri Matisse. Jack
knew he was really from Daly City, a fog-bound BART stop
between the airport and downtown. But that didn't matter.
Neither did whatever Henri chose to call himself. What did
matter was him waking up again.

Jack was sitting in a chair beside his hospital bed. The days
in the ICU had dropped Henri down to a flyweight, maybe even
an atomweight. He hadn't regained consciousness since the brief
moment he'd smiled at Katie. Jack kept on talking as if they were
seated together at Golden Gate Fields watching the El Camino
Real Derby.

"It's a blue pearl," he said. "The plan is to lure Jonathan
Gossamer with the groundwater basin. He's smart but he's even
greedier. I could use your advice on where the pitfalls might lie."

Jack shifted his weight. The chair creaked. "And what's with the photographs you wanted me to find? The banknotes and ATM receipt was a better trail than Hansel and Gretel's, but I'm still lost in the woods about their importance. Who are the mother and child?"

The rhythmic whoosh of the mechanical ventilator remained unchanged. The whir of the IV infusion pump didn't vary. The digital numbers and graphs flashing on the bedside monitor stayed within a narrow band.

Jack sucked his teeth and checked his watch. He'd been there for more than an hour. "Want to see them?"

He was fishing the purple envelope from his pocket when the red indicator light on the pulse oximeter clamped to Henri's right index finger stopped blinking. A few seconds passed before it started up again. The heart rate numbers on the bedside monitor increased. 75. 85. 100. The stairway graph climbed right along with them. Henri's eyelids flickered. Jack leaned over the bed and stared into his pale blue eyes. The pupils were still fixed and dilated.

"Henri, it's Jack. Can you hear me? Can you hear me?"

The old forger's eyelashes fluttered. Slowly. Surely. And then he blinked. The pupils suddenly constricted to the size of pinheads. Henri's lips pursed around the ventilator's mouth-piece. Jack snatched a washcloth from the overbed table, dipped a corner into a glass of water, and dabbed his lips. Henri moaned and used his eyes to urge Jack to wet his lips again.

"Attaboy. Welcome back."

The surge of activity on the monitors brought Taylor S. clomping in from her station on the other side of the glass.

"Now, don't you have the magic touch." She pushed Jack out of the way and adjusted the controls on the bedside machines and checked the central line feeding liquids and drugs into Henri's veins. "Stay awake a little longer this time, honey. You got a visitor." She clucked, smoothed the thin blanket over his frail body, and then said to Jack, "Don't wear him out, you hear?"

"Can you remove the ventilator so he can talk?"

Her bouffant waggled. "Dr. Heartache has to order it first, but I can ask him next time he does rounds. I'll go get a sponge bath tray."

Jack removed the three photographs from the purple envelope and held up the one of the woman and little girl.

"Is she the dancer from the cruise ship you told me about, Madhuri? Does this mean she didn't kill herself like you were told?"

Henri didn't respond.

Jack held the photo closer. "That would make this photo thirty years old. Is she still alive? Who sent it to you? What do they want?"

The ventilator whirred. Henri gurgled.

Jack showed the picture of the little girl playing in a front yard with mountains behind. "Is this India? Are those the Himalayas?"

Slowly—achingly slowly—Henri closed his eyes and then opened them again. Jack shuffled the deck to reveal the third photograph, the close-up of the little blue-eyed girl with the silver barrette.

"Tell me, Henri. Is this your daughter?"

The old forger struggled to lift his right hand. The exertion triggered the bedside monitor alarm. The graph tracking his heartbeat zigzagged wildly. The ventilator kicked into high gear to pump more oxygen. The alarm screamed. He aimed his index finger. The red light on the pulse oximeter blinked faster and faster before his arm fell back and his eyes closed.

≈

JACK INTERCEPTED Taylor S. as she walked back with the sponge bath tray. "Can we talk for a second?"

"Sure, handsome. What is it?"

"It has to do with Henri."

"I told you I'd ask Dr. Heartthrob about the ventilator. Who knows, all goes well, they could move Henri into his own room."

"Actually it's about the private nurses who were caring for him. One of them was murdered. Alison Kanasis. You may have heard about it."

Taylor S. nearly dropped the tray. "That girl worked for Henri? It's the talk of the hospital. I hope the police find who did it and fast. It's giving all us a fright."

"No doubt. Another one of Henri's nurses took the news so hard she OD'd on tranquilizers and wound up here in psyche on a seventy-two hour hold."

Taylor S. grimaced. "I hate hearing that kind of stuff. The poor thing."

"That's what I wanted to ask you. I know her. Is there a way I can check up on her? If I talk to her it might help."

"Still being the Good Samaritan, huh? I've never worked that ward, but I understand they have strict rules about visitors. Some of those patients are crazy. I mean real-life bat-shit crazy." Her bouffant tilted. "I don't think so, handsome."

"I'll level with you. She knows something about the other nurse's murder but she's not telling the cops because she's too scared. She'll tell me though. She trusts me. Then I can tell the cops and they can do their job and get the killer off the streets. That'd be a good thing for every nurse."

Taylor S. fiddled with the three colored pens hanging around her neck. "I do know somebody who works that floor. He used to do EMT before coming over here. I guess I could ask him. What's her name?"

Jack gave it to her. "Katie's right. You are the best."

"Do tell."

ONE LENS of Rainey's red glasses was cracked. They'd been placed on a shelf but she couldn't have reached them if she tried. Velcro cuffs bound her wrists to the bed rails and a six-inch wide belt cinched across her chest pinned her to the mattress. No shampoo had touched her hair since Jack saw her last. The sheets were clammy and made her skin appear even more washed out.

Jack pulled up a chair so he wouldn't have to stand. The orderly told him he'd appear less threatening that way. He also cautioned him to speak in a soothing voice and not make any sudden moves.

"You're safe now, Rainey. Everybody here wants to help you."

Her eyes darted like fish. Tooth marks pocked her lips. "Jack?"

"Yeah, it's me all right. You're safe."

She trembled and then the words came spilling out. "They wouldn't believe me. I told them I was in danger but they wouldn't do a thing. And I couldn't sleep. And I could hear footsteps. Somebody breathing. Somebody clawing at my door. Knocking on my window. Someone trying to get in and kill me."

"But you're safe now," Jack said.

"I told the police he'd murder me too but they wouldn't believe me."

"I believe you."

"I don't like it here. They hurt me. They give me things." She struggled against the restraints. "Look at me? I want to go home. Oh god, I can't go home. I can't go anywhere. He'll kill me like he killed Alison. Like he killed Ji-min."

"We don't know that she's dead," Jack said. "She could be hiding."

Rainey started to thrash. Jack kept from reaching over and putting his hand on her arm. The orderly warned him against touching her.

"You know me. You can trust me. I came from Henri's room. He's here in the hospital too. He's awake. He finally came out of his coma. You can visit him as soon as you're ready. I know he'd love to see you. He cares about you."

Her gyrations slowed. "Henri?"

"Yes, Henri. Loveable old Henri."

"He... he's okay?"

"He's getting better every minute."

"That... that's good, isn't it?"

"It's very good. And you're going to be okay too. You're safe now."

"Are you sure?"

"Positive." He knew the IV bag was filled with some kind of cocktail aimed at countering what she'd taken but also to keep her calm.

She set her jaw. "He's going to kill me. I know it."

"No he's not. I won't let him."

"You won't?"

"I won't."

"The police wouldn't listen to me. The detective. What's his name?"

"Lieutenant Dolan. I'll listen to you. I'll believe you."

"You will?"

"Of course. I'm Henri's friend. He trusts me. You can trust me too."

"I don't know. I don't know what to think. I want out of here. I want it all to go away. I don't want him to hurt me anymore. Hurt anyone. I want him to..."

"You mean Jonathan Gossamer." Jack said it as if blowing out a candle. Soft. Steady. Quiet.

Her entire body tensed. She tried to bring her hands to her chest but the restraints prevented it. "How do you know that?"

"You told me, remember? You're safe now."

Teeth showed on her bottom lip again but she didn't bite down. "He used me. He broke my heart. Crushed it. Ugh."

"How did you meet him?"

"I told you about him?"

"When I came to see you. Why you won't read Charlotte Brontë again."

"I was at a bar. He picked me up. I told you about him?" she said again.

"You said you'd gone to restaurants and wine bars with him. He brought you that box of expensive wine you keep in your closet."

Her lip curled. "I wouldn't drink it if you paid me. I hate him."

"You said he was very interested in Henri. Did he say why?"

"I don't know. I don't think so. It was only... only conversation." She took a deep breath. "At least that's what I thought."

Jack sensed she was about to take a turn. He didn't have much time. The orderly had agreed to give him only a few minutes. He rolled the dice.

"When did you find out he was also seeing Alison?"

Rainey moaned. Jack thought he'd lost her but she shook it off. "I always knew there were other women. There had to be. The way he looks. Acts. All his money. I told myself I didn't care as long as I didn't see him with them or know their names. What an idiot." She jerked her hands again to try and slap herself. The bed rail made a sound like the chord of an upright bass being plucked.

"Alison told you?"

"Yes. Not his name right away, but it wasn't too hard for both of us to figure it out. Ugh. We were both idiots and now she's dead."

Rainey seemed to sink deeper into the mattress.

"What about Ji-min? Was he seeing her too?"

"I don't know. I doubt it. She's so serious."

"Did you and Jonathan ever talk about the photographs in the purple envelope?"

"I don't think so. I don't remember. Why?"

He didn't have an answer.

Rainey started growing agitated again. "I don't need these restraints. I'm not going to hurt myself. When can I get out of here? Could you go tell a doctor I want to leave?"

"Sure, Rainey. I'll go see what I can do. One last thing, and this is important. Did Jonathan ever mention a woman named Grace?"

"I don't know any Grace."

"He never asked you about Grace Millefiore?"

Her voice rose. "I told you I don't know anybody named Grace. Why don't you believe me?"

"I do believe you. Okay, calm down. Everything's okay. I'll go find a doctor. I'll come back and see you real soon."

"I tell you I don't know any Grace," she shrieked and struggled against the restraints. "That's what I told him and he wouldn't believe me. He asked me and I told him I didn't know her, and he kept asking me over and over again. And I kept telling him I didn't know her. And then he called me a stupid fat pig and walked out."

"It's okay, Rainey. You're safe. He's not going to hurt you ever again."

Rainey struggled but finally got her breath under control. Her eyes still looked wild though. "Who's Grace? Did he kill her too?"

19

The regulars were occupying their regular tables at The Pier Inn when Jack arrived. Hark and Wonder Boy were bumping foreheads across the bar.

"We were talking about Tully and the Article 7 he hangs with," Hark said by way of greeting. "The guy you saw driving the jacked-up pickup."

"Orange face."

"He looks like that on account of pills." Hark was drinking something on the rocks in a tall glass. "He's hooked on those super antibiotics the medics dole out like candy. Reason why everybody calls him Z-Pak."

"Azithromycin," Jack said.

"Yeah, he thinks they'll protect him from bugs. He's got a giant phobia about scorpions. The ones in the 'Stan are especially nasty. They're called deathstalkers."

"Guess he didn't read the fine print about how overdosing on antibiotics will make him more drug resistant when he really needs it. A common cold could knock him off."

"He's dumb through and through. It's a wonder he passed the ASVAB test they give dudes trying to enlist. Somehow he got himself shipped over but didn't last long before they threw his ass out for burning down his own tent. Same thing as shooting yourself in the foot."

"Firebugs. My old man used to tell me about them. Z-Pak sounds like the kind who'd get off throwing a gasoline bomb at a wine cellar, burn down a barn with a kid and animals in it."

Wonder Boy returned with an Anchor Steam. Jack took a long pull of the beer as if it could wash out the taste of the psyche ward. Hark rattled the ice in his glass.

Jack said, "You find out where Gossamer lives?"

"I tailed him to a garage in one of those fancy new condo towers near the Transbay Terminal. Gate closed behind them when they entered so I had to break off."

"You need a s-s-special s-s-security pass to enter," Wonder Boy said. "I can s-s-score you one if you need it."

Jack saluted Wonder Boy with the beer. "I may take you up on that. Were you able to get any intel on the third nurse, Ji-min?"

The statistician extraordinaire went to work with his bar towel on an invisible watermark. "S-s-she has a very clean s-s-screen."

"Too clean?"

"S-s-some might think s-s-so. Her s-s-school registration is light on details. I can s-s-show you a copy."

"And before she became a nurse?"

"Only a rent application for an apartment in the Marina. S-s-she moved in a month ago. Used an Arizona driver's license."

"Everyone knows you can print those yourself. But what do you expect from a state that doesn't require a permit for concealed carry. What about a social?"

"S-s-she didn't list one and I can't find it."

"If you can't find it that means it doesn't exist. It also means the cops aren't having any luck tracking her down either."

"They entered her into the federal NamUs database, and they've issued a missing persons flyer with her s-s-student ID photo on it," Wonder Boy said.

Hark asked, "What about the nurse who tried to whack herself?"

"Rainey. She told me she had a thing for Gossamer. Said so did Alison, the dead nurse."

"So why isn't Terry Dolan all up in his face. She must have named him."

"I'm sure she did but he may be chalking it up as a "he said, she said" now that she's in psyche. The brass could've ordered him to stand down too, considering who Gossamer was partying with at the Fairmont. I'll bet you he's written some pretty sizable campaign checks."

"Do you want me to find out to whom and how much?" Wonder Boy asked.

"On the QT, sure. And while you're at, there's something else I need." He pulled out the purple envelope. "Can you track down this PO Box and find out who it's registered to? There's no zip code."

Wonder Boy glanced at the envelope. It was all he needed to commit it to memory.

Hark finished his drink. "So what's next, *ese*? We wait till the ducks all in a row or do we get to start playing?"

Jack drained his beer. "Usually I'd say wait but we don't have the time, not with the likes of Tully and Z-Pak on the loose. Let's push it some and see what develops."

Hark grinned. "Now you're talking. I like it when shit develops."

THE CITROËN's windshield wipers were clacking double time as

Jack left the Pier. He ran two yellow lights on Broadway before dropping down to Cow Hollow. Union Street was jammed despite the rain and the odds of finding a parking spot were slim. He pulled in front of a fire hydrant and slapped his old man's shield on the dashboard to buy him a pass from the meter reader. The store he was after was across the street so he made a dash between cars. A woman was flipping over the open sign when he got there.

"Hang on," he said. "I'm supposed to meet my wife. Traffic was a nightmare."

"She's waiting for you inside." Her smile was professional. "You might work on your timing if you don't want to be late for the main event."

Jack sucked his teeth and hurried inside. Something squeaked beneath his foot. He jumped and nearly knocked over a display of teddy bears. "What the...?"

"It's only a Marvin the Moose. But I'd give anything if I had a video. Some man of steel you are." Katie imitated a high pitch shriek. She was test-driving a white wicker rocking chair.

Jack took a bow. "Always happy to amuse." He glanced around. The store was crowded with high chairs and changing tables. "You sure we're going to need all this stuff?"

"A couple of basics is all." Katie let it percolate. "For starters."

"Guess it's a good thing we live in a warehouse."

He helped her up and she led him on a tour. The woman with the fixed grin intercepted them at a display of blankets.

"Boy or girl?"

Katie winked. "We're big on surprises."

"How quaint."

"Do you have anything in basic black?" Jack said.

That unfroze the woman's smile.

Katie had a list and they checked it off in thirty minutes. The crib, car seat, and stroller would be delivered.

It was still raining when they readied to leave. "Perry's is on the next block," Jack said. "We may as well grab some dinner while we're here."

"I've always loved their martinis," Katie said.

"I'll let you have my olive."

"See? You're a natural born provider."

They shared an umbrella up the street. The hostess seated them at a table for four. Jack eyed the empty chairs and muttered, "I'm going to be surrounded."

Katie laughed. "One at a time, okay?"

They ordered grilled salmon and split an arugula, spinach, and beet salad. Katie told him she'd stopped by the hospital and learned Henri was making remarkable progress.

"Taylor said they will take him off the ventilator any day now. Their main concern is neurological damage to his legs. He didn't respond well to a bedside test."

"Where they poke pins in your feet. But they told you it's too early to tell for sure, right?"

"Yes, but it got me thinking. I should add physical therapy to my offerings at the gyms. There's a real need for it especially given the age of all the baby boomers."

"That to go along with the prenatal exercise classes and stuff for little kids you're already planning. Womb to tomb. You're starting to sound like a socialist."

Katie was picking out the beets and eating them one by one. "It's called life cycle. It's in all the enterprise management books."

"I'll bet."

She finished the beets and started in on the greens. "You know what I couldn't help thinking when I saw Henri? How sad it is he doesn't have any family. I know we're like a son and daughter to him but still."

"Maybe he does."

"What do you mean?"

Jack hesitated but it was too late to take it back. "It's something I found in his safety deposit box. Some photographs." He told her about Madhuri.

"Do you really think she could still be alive and that's their daughter?"

"It seems unlikely but you never know."

"We'll have to find out. It could be just the medicine Henri needs."

She picked up the menu and checked to see if they had crème brûlée.

20

Rock solid was the image the Financial District money houses wanted to project but the truth was they were built on mud. San Francisco Bay once lapped all the way up to Montgomery Street and many of the downtown office buildings stood on fill that included the remains of clipper ships abandoned in place by gold-struck sailors. The latest wave of get-rich-quick fever was no less infectious as people worked the streets to cash in on tech, from investors who doubled down on apps designed by teenagers to food truck chefs serving twenty dollar tongue tacos and cornflake crusted chicken wraps.

Such a climate was perfect for hatching a con, and Jack could sense the hothouse atmosphere the moment he stepped into the lobby of Wine Futures, Inc. The layout was a model of a big store and the players were well-rehearsed. A troupe was fostering a hive of activity inside a glass-walled meeting room strategically placed behind the reception desk. The furniture was stylish, and Jack didn't need Henri LeConte to tell him the blue chip modern art paintings on the walls were fakes.

A receptionist dressed in stiletto heels and a skintight dress better suited for a night out clubbing stood beside the front desk. She wore a smile as big as the Ritz.

"Welcome to Wine Futures," she cooed.

Jack pasted on an appreciative grin. "I called earlier. I have an appointment with a Mr. Jonathan Gossamer."

She smiled right back as if they were sharing a suggestive joke or an icy shot of vodka. "Of course, you're his two o'clock. May I escort you to his suite?"

Jack followed her down a hall lined by a phalanx of closed doors. Muted voices came from behind each. He remembered using recordings to create the same effect.

Gossamer's office had a view of downtown and a sliver of the bay beyond, but despite the windows, the room was cool and gray as dusk. A temperature-controlled walk-in wine cellar occupied one side. The racks were filled floor to ceiling. Three monitors hung on the opposite wall. One was tuned to Bloomberg TV, the other to CNBC, and the third was a closed circuit loop of vineyards from around the world.

Gossamer stood at the window with his back to them. He wore a headset and was holding a three-way conversation, alternating between English, French, and Mandarin. He turned and acknowledged Jack with a wink. "Gentlemen, I need to sign off. Are we clear on the delivery dates? Very good. I look forward to confirmation of the wire transfers. Good-bye, Mr. Bennett. *Au revoir*, Monsieur Leclerc. *Zài jiàn*, Chen Xiansheng."

He removed the headset. "Mr. McCoul, is it? Jonathan Gossamer. A pleasure. Please have a seat. I understand you are interested in our portfolio of offerings." A tongue flicked across his lips.

"I am. I visited your website and read the prospectus but before I make any investment decisions I always like to look the managers in the eye and see what they're made of."

Gossamer leaned back in his chair. He was dressed the same

as he was the night at the Fairmont fundraiser, right down to the red Pumas on his feet. His hair was freshly trimmed and frosted. His thin face made Jack think of a scalpel.

"A very sound strategy that has no doubt served you well. I am happy to answer any questions you may have."

"Glad to hear it. The prospectus is long on superlatives and short on specifics. I need to know about rates of return and tax advantages."

"I see you are an experienced investor. May I ask what asset classes you are most comfortable with?"

"I make it a rule not to discuss the specifics of my holdings. Suffice to say they're balanced and diversified. Equities, commodities, real estate, and a few positions in private equity. That sort of thing."

"I see. A traditional strategy. You will find that while Wine Futures has commonalities with all of those, we are focused on a specific segment of the market to take advantage of an unprecedented growth opportunity. Our offerings are structured as closed-end funds. Each is a strategic mix of various strata of the wine industry. Production, distribution, marketing, and futures. For example, one of our portfolios invests solely in actual vintages with the goal of achieving maximum appreciation as the selections mature. We have a real estate portfolio comprised of both proven and new vineyards. It operates the same as a traditional REIT. You are familiar with real estate investment trusts? Of course you are." He wet his lips.

"That's what it says on your website but what it doesn't say is how your funds are benchmarked, how they're performing."

"That is because the Dow Jones and S&P 500 are not comparable indexes. Frankly, we see that as an advantage. We are market makers, not followers. In time others will use us as the benchmark. I can say with complete confidence that our returns match the top ten percent of all hedge funds. For the qualified investor, we also offer access to companies seeking private equity. Wineries are the new start-up, would not you agree? Our role is to find them before they become household brands. Naturally, there is greater risk but then again the rewards can be greater."

Jack pictured a televangelist, a motivational speaker, and a late night pitchman all rolled into one. "What's the minimum?" he asked brusquely.

Gossamer showed his teeth. "I do value frankness. It is one million dollars but the majority of our client partners have significant capacity so they invest accordingly. Obviously there must be a few restrictions on redemptions as timing and amounts are usually dictated by the market. We certainly would not want you to sell and miss out on an upcoming merger or acquisition that could provide a sizable boost in net asset value." The teeth gleamed brighter. "Maximizing profits and protecting you, the investor, is our number one goal."

A classic Madoff, Jack thought. "That sounds interesting but..." he made a show of looking around as if to confirm they were alone. "I'm actually interested in an asset class not listed on your website."

"Oh, and what would that be?"

"Water."

"I do apologize. My receptionist should have offered you a beverage the moment you arrived. How careless. I will ring her immediately. Still or sparkling?"

Jack's laugh was dismissive. "You know what California and the Bible have in common?"

"I do not, Mr. McCoul. Please enlighten me."

"The miracle of turning water into wine."

"Whatever gave you the idea Wine Futures is interested in investing in water?"

"My sources tell me you've been shopping for senior rights

in the Central Valley. That takes capital. A lot of it. And I'm willing to put some of mine up so you can purchase more. For the right return of course. I want to know what the buy-in rate is and if you have any problems with a trust based in the Cayman Islands as your newest investor."

The salesman's smile melted. "I am afraid you have been misinformed. Our firm is not active in that area nor do we have plans as such. What I can do is have one of my senior client advisors call you at a later date to discuss your financial goals and recommend a fund that would complement your existing portfolio."

Jack brushed off the brush-off. "If you're not selling, perhaps you'd be interested in buying."

"I was under the impression you were an investor. It would seem the purpose of our meeting was misconveyed, would not you agree? My receptionist will see you out."

"I am an investor and part of investing is selling."

Gossamer hesitated. "All right, for the sake of conversation what are you proposing to sell?"

"Groundwater. Enough to irrigate every vineyard in the Central Valley for years."

"Ridiculous, Mr. McCoul. That is utterly preposterous."

"That's what everyone thinks. But what they don't know is what I know. And that's the location of a forgotten basin that's flush with runoff thanks to El Niño."

"To repeat myself, ridiculous. All of the hydrogeological features in the state are mapped, tested, and retested on a regular basis. Given the years of drought any groundwater basins that showed even a glimmer of promise would most assuredly be under intense scrutiny with exploration and development poised to begin the moment they proved to be profitable." Gossamer stood. "Good day."

"Fine but don't say I didn't offer."

Jack didn't look back as he escorted himself to the reception area. Tully was waiting there. Jack walked up to him.

"You work here?"

Dental patients loaded up with Novocain showed more expression. Tully's eyes didn't even blink. "What do you want?"

"An answer to my question. Do you work here?"

Tully balanced on the balls of his feet. "And I said, what do you want?"

Jack slid his hand toward his inside breast pocket. Tully's hand automatically went to his hip. Jack extracted a parking ticket stub.

"Do you validate?"

～

THE TAIL STAYED three car lengths back. It was the pickup truck on steroids he'd seen in Clemens. Jack took a circuitous route to Golden Gate Park. He parked and entered the main exhibition hall of the California Academy of Sciences. He waited by the four-story rainforest terrarium to give Z-Pak time to catch up. The man's orange complexion was hard to miss in the crowd. Jack strolled through the exhibit rooms before taking the stairs down to the basement level.

Sharks patrolled above him and schools of fish swam alongside as he crossed through the acrylic aquarium tunnel. At the other end he paused at a door signed *Entomology* before entering. He closed it behind him. A minute later the door opened again.

Jack greeted Z-Pak by shoving an eight-inch-long scorpion in his face. Z-Pak shrieked and backed up fast. "What is that?"

"It's an emperor scorpion from West Africa. They've got drawers full of specimens in here." Jack wiggled the dried creature.

Z-Pak's eyes grew wide as he nervously surveyed the room. He stabbed his right hand behind him but an iron grip clamped around his wrist and wrenched it up to his shoulder blades.

"Ow!" he screamed

"Shut up or I'll snap it like a chicken wing," Hark said.

The big man held up the S&W 9mm he plucked from Z-Pak's holster. "Dude was definitely no scout in the 'Stan. You see that T. rex they got upstairs? It could've shadowed him and he still wouldn't've noticed."

Jack thrust the scorpion again. "You want to tell me why you're following me?"

The orange complexion darkened. "Suck it."

Hark wrenched Z-Pak's wrist higher. "Show some respect. We stick you in a drawer, by the time they find you, you'll be as dried out as the rest of the bugs."

"I'd listen to him if I were you," Jack said. "After two tours in Afghanistan, he wrote a recipe book on cooking insects. Let's try it again. Why are you following me?"

Hark gave another wrench for encouragement.

"Orders," Z-Pak gasped. "I do what I'm told."

"Okay, so now I'm the one giving the orders. Who told you to follow me?"

"Can't say."

"Can't or won't?" Jack stroked Z-Pak's nose with the scorpion's pinchers. "You want to see one from the Congo? Size of a sewer rat. One bite from it and you got liquid fire running through your veins before your bowels turn inside out. Messy."

Z-Pak shuddered again. "Okay, okay. My CO ordered it."

"Tully," Jack said.

"Yeah. Tully."

"Why'd he want me followed?"

"I dunno. He just did."

Hark gave him another wrench.

"Okay, okay. He wanted to see if you're for real or not. See if you're a cop or some kinda hustler trying to jack Mr. Gossamer around."

"Tully's not going to like it you getting caught like this. Maybe you should think of an early retirement plan."

"You're the one should be scared of Tully."

Hark wrenched Z-Pak's arm up to the base of his neck. "Other way around, *pendejo*. Tell your boy Tully he wants to scare somebody, he should look in the mirror after I get done with him. Be the biggest fright he ever sees." He gave him a shove.

Z-Pak stumbled forward. He held out his wrist. "Ow, I think you broke it."

Jack said, "Tell Jonathan Gossamer he should've taken my offer seriously. Now if he wants to play in the water with me, it's going to cost him a lot more than a million bucks. Of course the rewards will be that much higher too. You got that?"

"Maybe. I guess so."

"Go on. Get out of here."

Z-Pak said, "What about my weapon?"

Hark dangled the S&W 9mm from his pinkie. "What about it?"

"A soldier never leaves his weapon on the field."

"You were never a soldier. They should've washed you out before they wasted a uniform." Hark spit at Z-Pak's feet. "I won't leave it on the field but I will throw it in the shark tank out there. You want it, you swim for it."

They watched Z-Park scuttle away.

"That ought to send Goss the message we're players," Hark said.

"Signed, sealed, and delivered," Jack said.

He put the emperor scorpion back in the drawer among even larger ones.

21

"Have you thought of any names yet?"

Katie asked it while lying on her side. She was spooning against Jack and held his palm against her stomach. Rain was drumming against the window and tiny fists were drumming against her womb.

"Muhammad Ali if it's a boy, Laila Ali if it's a girl."

"There's lots of movement because babies start exercising their lungs during the third trimester."

"You sure it's not because we were exercising tonight?"

"Sex during pregnancy is very healthy. At least sixteen of the one hundred Kama Sutra positions are expressly for pregnant women. Just now? That one's called the spider."

"What a tangled web we weaved."

Katie laughed. "Smart aleck."

They listened to the rain and drifted in and out of the twilight that exists right before slumber. Jack tried to keep his thoughts away from Henri and the nurses, but it was hard. There were too many loose ends. Since the run-in with Z-Pak, he'd received an e-mail from Do Pray telling him all the information on Sabbia Plain had been uploaded into the State Water

Resources' database with a tracker that would ping the moment someone conducted a search. Cicero Broadshank also checked in. He gave a longwinded description of how a real estate transaction using a quitclaim was typically used when speed and minimal legal oversight was desired but once executed could serve as both evidence and indictment. Wonder Boy called too. He was still trying to nail down the owner of the PO Box, but word on the street was someone was collecting intel on Jack and was paying top dollar for it.

Jack hadn't heard anything more from Terry. He guessed the homicide cop's investigation ran into a dead end. He considered and then rejected telling him about Jonathan Gossamer. While he knew the punk in Pumas was responsible, he still had no evidence that would tie him to Alison's death and Ji-min's disappearance. The big question remained why.

Patience was a con artist's best trait. Plays were like fine wine. They needed time to mature and reach their full potential. His rule was "You rush it, you flush it." Speed bred mistakes. Mistakes spooked marks. Worse, they attracted attention from the law. Jack's most successful plays had always been long cons but sometimes he didn't have that luxury. This felt like one of them. Murder had a way of throwing everything off.

Katie's purrs turned into snores. They were nearly as loud as Chagall's. She'd told him snoring was a by-product of pregnancy because of increased swelling of the nasal passages. She'd taken to drinking a homemade remedy of soy milk, honey, turmeric, and red onion before bed every night. Jack countered with two fingers of Jameson. It also helped silence the nagging voices in his head begging for answers to who were the mother and child in Henri's photographs.

BEES, big ones, were buzzing all around. Jack slapped at them but the swarm grew louder. He bolted awake before they could sting. His phone was skittering on top of the nightstand. He scooped it up as he slid out of bed, hopped over the slumbering poodle, and thumbed accept when he reached the other room.

"Speak."

Silence responded and then a murmur and then a mumble and then a cry. "Will you help me? Please?"

"Who is this?"

"You are Jack McCoul, yes? Henri's friend?"

"That's right. Who's this?"

"Ji-min. I am one of his nurses. You are his friend, yes?"

Jack was wide awake now. "Where are you?"

"I am hiding. I am frightened. I need help. Please?"

"Of course. Where are you?"

"I do not want anyone to find me."

"If you don't tell me where you are I can't help you. Call the police. They'll protect you."

"No police. I do not trust them."

"They want to help you."

"I trust you because you are Henri's friend. You will help me, yes?"

Jack sucked his teeth. "Okay, why don't you come here? I'll give you my address."

"No. It is too dangerous to travel. They are looking for me everywhere."

"Who's looking for you?"

The pause was long. "You will help me, please?"

The kitchen clock showed midnight. "If I'm going to come to you, I'll need to know where."

Ji-min didn't answer. Jack strained to listen but couldn't make out any of the background noises.

"Look, I helped Rainey and now she's safe. I can get you to safety too."

Ji-min said, "All right but I am not in San Francisco. I am on Henri's houseboat. I kept a key. Can you come quick? Please?"

"It will take me at least an hour to get there. Stay inside. Keep the lights off. Don't open the door. I'll knock once and only once and then I'll let myself in. Okay?"

"Please hurry, yes?"

"I'm on my way."

22

Foghorns bellowed. Headlights boomeranged off swirling vapors. Droplets the size of water balloons lost their grip on the Golden Gate Bridge's suspension cables and plonked the car roof. The Citroën's wipers were fighting a losing battle. So was the defroster, even though it was cranked on high.

Jack cracked the windows and tasted salt. He had no way of knowing if Ji-min was alone, had someone holding a gun to her head, or was working with Jonathan Gossamer to set him up. He knew the smart move would be to call Hark for backup, but sometimes speed was more important than strategy. This seemed like one of them. He drove faster.

Sausalito was buttoned up tight. Even the seagulls were asleep. Jack turned off the lights and ignition and coasted into the lot on Gate 5 Road. He made the drive in thirty minutes as he knew he could. Surprise wasn't the only thing he was counting on. A thirty-two-inch red and black alloy slugger he swung when he played shortstop at San Francisco State rested on the seat next to him. It was NCAA approved. Metal bats were preferred over ash because they were safer. Colleges weren't thinking about bad guys on the receiving end.

Jack made sure the dome light was off before opening the car door. He closed it silently and gripped the big stick and walked softly. Up ahead Henri's houseboat was blacked out. The only noise came from wavelets scrubbing against the boat slips and a clanging bell at the end of the dock. No way he was going to use the front door like he told Ji-min. Instead, he stepped on the deck of the houseboat belonging to the David Crosby look-alike with the octopus sticker. Jack hoped he and his wife and their six cats were sound sleepers. He soft-shoed across and hopped onto the deck of its neighbor and crossed that one too. From there he dropped onto the stern of Henri's houseboat without causing the barge to rock. No front door for him either. He opened a hatch that led to the hold and slipped inside.

The hold was as black as the devil's heart the priests used to lecture him about at St. Joseph's. They warned his would turn the same color if he didn't give up the wages of sin. Jack went straight out and got the image tattooed on his shoulder. Later, when he was deep in the life, he had it re-inked as a shamrock. He'd rather be lucky than bad.

He crouched in the hold and listened. Nothing. After five minutes he crept forward. There was another hatch door that led to Henri's stateroom. Jack gritted his teeth, opened it, and waited. Again he listened. Nothing. He clicked on a penlight and shined it around. Empty. He clicked it off, waited, and then moved forward to the door that led to the main room. He paused and then opened it. He held his breath and listened. He heard the sound of another heartbeat over the hum of the refrigerator. One other not more.

"Ji-min," he called softly. "Are you all right?"

A voice murmured back. He flicked on the penlight and aimed it at the couch. The narrow beam found her. Ji-min was sitting with her hands folded primly on her lap. She blinked. Jack went to the wall switch and flicked on the overhead light. He turned toward her. She was dressed in a dark blue pantsuit. The blouse was ivory.

"Jack McCoul? Henri's friend?" she said.

He started to reply.

That's when the door to the houseboat's head swung open behind him. That's when the barge rocked. That's when the lights clicked off and Jack tumbled deep down dark.

SMOKE CHOKED the air and wind howled through the open doors of the helitanker. A shoulder harness held Jack to a jump seat but the straps were too big for his boyish frame. He could hear his father yelling through the headset. Gavin was in the cockpit braying like a donkey every time the pilot steered the chopper between the Oakland skyscrapers ringing Lake Merritt, scooped up another giant bucket of water, and hauled it to the East Bay hills to dump on an inferno that was devouring neighborhoods and leaving ash and charred corpses in its wake.

The boom, boom, boom from cars detonating from the firestorm pounded through the headset and Jack could feel the concussions in his chest. Bile rose in his throat as the helitanker banked steeply between towering black twisters choked with cinders and soot. Debris pelted the rotors and banged against the fuselage. He wanted to scream but didn't want to give his father the satisfaction. When the call had come from OFD asking all Bay Area cities for mutual aid, Gavin was in the middle of beating Jack for trying to stop him from slapping around his wife. He gave his son one last cuff upside the head. "It's time to cut the apron strings, *boyo*. Watch and learn how a real man works."

Gavin manned the chopper's front-mounted water cannon while Jack rode in the bay with a crewman charged with minding the winch controlling the 2,500-gallon bucket. The pilot and crewman never questioned why a boy was on board, such was the firefighters' code. Jack tried closing his eyes but that only made the rollercoaster ride worse. The chopper climbed and dove. It bucked and spun. Over and over again.

The sky was the color of fresh bruises and a miasma of burnt flesh and melted rubber hung over Oakland like a plague as they made their final run. The chopper strained with a full bucket as it followed Broadway east toward the Caldecott Tunnel. The fire had jumped two freeways, laid waste to Upper Rockridge, scorched the headstones in Mountain View Cemetery, and was thundering toward downtown.

Wind howling through the Golden Gate rushed across the bay and smacked the chopper at the same time a mushroom cloud of smoke and flame erupted beneath from a grove of oily eucalyptus trees. The collision slammed the chopper and sent it spiraling out of control. Cockpit alarms shrieked and the pilot's swears quickly turned into pleas for Jesus. The craft tumbled onto its side and Jack was plucked from his loose harness and hurled out the open bay. He plummeted to earth only to be bungeed by a safety line knotted around his waist.

Jack grabbed onto the umbilical cord and held on tight. Flying like a broken kite, he zigzagged through the smoke-filled air, banging repeatedly into the fuselage, caught between the thwapping of the murderous top rotor and the power saw whine of the tail's. Embers singed his clothes. Debris slapped his face. Still he wouldn't let go. The pilot finally righted the craft. The winch crewman grabbed the safety line and hauled Jack back in. He slammed him into his seat, buckled the harness, and gave him the thumbs up.

When they landed, Gavin greeted Jack with a bray. "You see

me fire that cannon? I knocked the shit out of flames a hundred feet high. That's the way it's done, *boyo*. What do you say about your old man now?"

The ground was spinning and it was all Jack could do to stand upright. He tried to think of something biting to say but couldn't trust his voice so he reared back, put his shoulder into it, and threw a punch.

LIGHTS FLASHED. Sounds crackled. Jack could hear his father's taunts as he drove his fist toward his jaw but it met a hand instead.

"Easy, *ese*. You okay?"

Jack's eyes flickered. Hark cupped his fist in one hand and held his Beretta M9 in the other. Other hands cradled his head. Soft hands. He rested in a lap. A soft lap. Jack looked up.

Sparks flew from Katie's emerald eyes. "Who did this to you?"

Jack struggled to sit. A wave of vertigo rushed in and his stomach heaved. He squinted to ward off the light. His gaze went straight to the couch.

"Where's Ji-min?"

"Who's Ji-min?" Katie asked.

"One of Henri's student nurses. The new one."

"You were alone when we got here," she said

Jack rocked onto his knees and crawled toward the couch. He patted the seat cushions. "She was right here."

Katie exchanged looks with Hark. "Well, she's not now, babe. She must have left after she hit you."

"Ji-min didn't hit me..." He stopped himself. His eyes met Hark's who extended the Beretta and started checking doors. Jack said to Katie, "How did you know I was here?"

"Grace called me."

It was like a second slug from the bat. "How did she get your number?"

"I gave it to her when we met at the hospital. She invited me out to their vineyard, and we were going to check calendars."

Jack probed the back of his head. A mushy lump the size of a golf ball was sprouting. "She say how she knew I was here?"

"A man called her."

"He give a name?"

"All he said was you were at Henri's and hurt. Maybe he's the one who hit you. What's this all about?"

"What did Grace say you were supposed to do about it?"

"She sounded worried. Grace said it would take her two hours to get here. She thought I should call the police."

"But you called Hark instead."

"Really, babe. I wasn't born yesterday. How's your head?"

Jack rubbed it. "Takes a lickin' keeps on tickin'."

Hark returned. "Nobody home."

Jack hooked a thumb at Katie. "You brought her here not knowing what to expect?"

"You know how she gets, 'mano. Like a mama tiger. All due respect."

"Don't I know it."

"He did try to talk me out of coming," Katie said. "You never answered me. What's all this about anyway?"

"Trouble," Jack said as he eyed the couch. Ji-min wasn't the only thing missing. So was his bat. "Big trouble."

23

The rain let up and Grace was in the vineyard checking for damage. Eddie remained on guard at the house while Chaco led Jack to her.

"Thanks," he said. "I got it from here."

She wore rubber boots and a man's felt hat and carried a pair of red handled pruners that she used to snip dead canes and broken tendrils. The cuttings fell to the ground.

"I'm glad to see you're okay," she said by way of greeting. "Was last night a false alarm?"

Jack picked up a cutting. "You tell me."

"All I know is a man said you were at Henri's and needed help, so I called your wife. Did she call the police?"

"You didn't recognize his voice?"

She snipped a withered tendril. "No and he didn't give me time to ask. What happened?"

"It was a setup. One of Henri's nurses called me. She said she was hiding on his houseboat and needed help. I snuck on board and got blindsided for my trouble. By the time I came to she was gone and so was whoever sapped me."

Grace kept snipping as she listened.

"You don't seem very upset that someone nearly turned off my lights for good," he said.

Grace faced him. The sun glinted off the curved blades of the pruner. "You're a tough guy, Jack. When we were together, I had to teach myself not to worry about you or I couldn't've done the things we did. What were you and Henri doing to bring all this on?"

"Nothing. We're both retired from the life."

"It must've been something since she was on Henri's boat and you're the one she called." Grace went back to pruning.

Jack said, "Whoever set me up got what they wanted."

"And what's that?"

"Leverage. They took something I brought with me."

"You're not telling me everything," she said.

"Ji-min, that's her name. Or at least it's the name's she's been using. She's been hiding out for a while. She isn't Henri's only nurse. There are three. One was murdered. The second nurse? She swallowed a bottle of tranquilizers because she got so scared about something."

Grace faced him again. "Okay, now you are scaring me. There's a murderer loose and Henri's nurses are the victims?"

"There's more." Jack bent the cutting and held both ends. He wished it was a divining rod that could point to truth. "Two of them were dating Jonathan Gossamer. He grilled them about Henri. He asked if Henri ever talked about you. Gossamer was pretty insistent."

Grace let the pruners fall to her side. When she spoke, her voice was a mix of sadness and frustration.

"Gossamer's been setting Stefan and me up for a while. He must've learned Henri and I are friends so he got close to the nurses to find something out about me he could use to force us to sell him our water rights."

"That's one explanation." Jack let it hang.

"What else could it be? He wants our water."

"But why kill a nurse, threaten another. A murder is the quickest way to deep-six a con."

"Maybe he didn't do it. Maybe it was his bodyguard. Maybe he likes killing. Maybe Gossamer plans to have Stefan and me killed and didn't want any loose ends that could tie him to us. I don't know."

"What could he get on you for leverage?" Jack waited. When she didn't answer, he said, "If Gossamer was threatening to tell Stefan about your past all you had to do was confess. Stefan would forgive you in an instant. No more lever."

"I suppose." Her voice was low and drifting.

"Level with me, Grace. What aren't you telling me?"

She hesitated. "I've told you what's important."

"That's not good enough. You know who lives in the details. Forgetting that is a ticket to prison or hell." Jack blew out air. "When was the last time you spoke to Henri?"

"I've seen him a couple of times since I came back."

"I'm surprised Henri never told me."

"That's because I asked him not to."

"How come?"

"Because he told me you were married. Because..." She looked down at her boots. They were splattered with mud. "Because I didn't want to hurt you again."

Jack closed the gap and wrapped his arms around her. He could feel all that they once had flow between them, both the good and the bad, but most of all the dangerous. He could hear the past calling him, feel the moment, sense the present, but what he couldn't see was the future.

CHACO WAS SITTING on the front porch when they returned to the house. Eddie's truck was gone. So was Stefan's SUV.

"What gives?" Jack said.

"Mr. Fabro, he got a call. He said he had to go meet someone. He didn't want Eddie to go so he drove himself. Eddie followed in his rig. He just called. Mr. Fabro, he's at a bar over in Lodi. Eddie poked his head in. He was at a table talking to two dudes. When Mr. Fabro spotted him he ordered him to go wait outside. He treated him like he was an illegal. Hey, we trying to help out here but there's no call for that."

"I'll go get him," Jack said.

Grace said, "I'll come with you."

"Better if you didn't. Be easier all the way around if Stefan doesn't think we're ganging up on him. Chaco, you good?"

"No problem, man. I can handle whatever comes up the drive myself." He lifted his shirt tail to reveal the automatic tucked in his waistband.

Grace huffed and went inside and let the door slam behind her. Chaco told Jack where the bar was. He got in the Citroën and made tracks.

The sun was still short of setting but the sky was already tinged with pink. Jack was on the two-lane highway heading west. The old Creedence track about being stuck in Lodi kept playing in his head. He'd always hated the song. He passed a field planted with grapevines. Silver ribbons fluttered from stakes, leftover scarecrows from last year's crop. Water ran in ditches controlled by sluice gates. A red-tailed hawk perched on a telephone pole.

His phone buzzed and his answer was gruff. "Speak."

"Jack?"

"How you doing Deputy Santos?"

"I was wondering if we could meet."

"You find something out?"

"Maybe. I'm at the major crimes unit in Stockton. I've been doing some research into what we talked about. Are you in San Francisco? We could meet halfway."

"Actually I'm out your way. I got something to do first. Give me a couple of hours and I can swing by the station."

"No, that won't work. I don't want people to—"

"I get it. Is there another place?"

"I have some work I need to finish up here. How's nine o'clock? There's a side road off the highway."

"Works for me."

She gave him the milepost and hung up.

Ten minutes later Jack found the bar on the outskirts of Lodi. Only a few cars were in the parking lot. He pulled between Stefan's SUV and Eddie's pickup.

"He's still in there," Eddie said.

"What about the men he was with?"

"They split a few minutes ago."

"What were they driving?"

"A black Lincoln crossover. You want the plate numbers?"

Jack said, "The driver have a beard and look like a hitter? The other guy wearing red sneakers?"

"Yeah, what's up with that look?"

"I'll go get Fabro. You can head back to the ranch, okay?"

"You'll want to take his keys. Last time I looked he was getting quite a load on. Chaco and me can fetch his ride later."

Jack went inside. The lounge was lit by neon beer signs. Country western was playing low. A couple of solitary drinkers hunched at the bar but kept several stools between them. *Who said no man is an island?* Jack thought. The bartender had old biker written all over him but Jack guessed he'd traded his Harley in for a three wheeler years ago. His muscles had slid into fat and there were more liver spots on his skull than on a springer spaniel.

Jack hooked a thumb at Stefan who was slouched at a table in the corner. "What's my friend over there drinking?"

"Double Bulleits. Neat. You matching him I'll pour you a pair. He told me not to let the well run dry."

"The only thing you better bring us is a glass of water."

The bartender puffed out his chest, but all that did was swell his man boobs. "This is a business. We sell booze. He orders, I'm filling it. Got it, partner?"

"There's two choices here," Jack said.

"Yeah and who's gonna tell me what they are?"

"Me, don't you know? Ice or no ice in the water."

He went to the table. "Come on, Stefan. Time to go home."

The winemaker looked up from a tumbler of bourbon. "You? You've got some nerve. You slept with my wife, you bastard. I'm going to knock your head off."

"No you're not. Come on, I'll give you a ride."

Stefan spanked the table. The glass jumped and brown liquid slopped over the rim. "You're sleeping with her now. I know you are. You bastard."

Jack sighed. He hated drunks. "Who told you that, Jonathan Gossamer?"

"It's true. I ought to kill you." He clutched the rest of his drink and downed it. It made him cough.

"That's what Gossamer wants you to do. You get thrown in prison and he'll walk away with your water. Don't believe him, believe your wife. She told you the truth. We were an item once but that was long before she fell in love with you. There's nothing between us. Nothing. Understand?"

"I don't believe you."

"I don't care if you do or not. I really don't. But you're a fool to believe the guy trying to steal your water. Don't let him work you like this. Don't give him that edge."

"He's got proof. He told me."

"And Trump's got hairspray. Grace is worried sick about you. I told her I'd bring you home and that's what I'm going to do. Easy is always better than hard. You coming or am I carrying?"

Fabro stared at his glass for a long time. Tears tinged his bleary eyes. "I'll drive myself."

"No you won't. The bartender told me he already took away your keys."

"Uh-uh." He reached into his pocket. "See, I got them right here."

Jack's move was so quick the keys didn't even jingle as he palmed them. "You ever ridden in a Citroën? No? You're in for a treat."

He poured Stefan into the front seat, got him buckled in, and whispered a word of thanks when the car started right up. Evening was coming on as he hit the highway and drove east. His passenger leaned against the door and moaned.

"You got a good thing. Don't blow it," Jack said.

Fabro said, "I fell in love with her the moment I met her. I'd never known anybody like her before. She... She turned me down flat, told me she wasn't interested. I told her okay, that it was okay if we kept it as friends but the whole time it wasn't okay."

Jack didn't want to hear any of it. He debated turning on the radio. Crank it up loud. He'd even listen to the damn Creedence song.

"I'd heard all the rumors and I didn't care." Fabro hiccuped. "The old women on the *estancias* were always gossiping about *la gringa*. Who she was. Where she came from. What she'd done. They said she was a movie star right out of the *telenovelas* on rehab because of drugs. I didn't care. They said she was a rich man's wife hiding until the divorce settled. I didn't care. They said she was *el presidente's* mistress and had his child and gave it to the nuns. They said they'd seen the proof that she'd recently borne a child. I didn't care because I love her." He started to sob.

The moon barely cleared the Sierra. The light shined directly onto the highway. Jack mistook it for the headlights of a car speeding straight at him. He didn't turn the wheel. He didn't care.

24

Grace was nervous. Jack had seen her play the part before but now it seemed for real. She fussed over them when they arrived. Jack helped Stefan into the house, propping him up with one arm and carrying his cane for him.

"A couple of aspirins and a good night's sleep he'll be right as rain," Jack said. "You might want to check his chest. He could have popped a stitch when he leaned out the window to hurl."

"Can you help me get him to the bedroom?"

They stretched him on the bed. It was the color and texture of a cumulus cloud with plump pillows sheathed in white and matching sheets and duvet. Stefan sank into it and started snoring.

Jack wanted to get the hell out of there but it was as if Grace read his thoughts.

"Don't leave before we have a chance to talk, okay?" She started pulling off her husband's shoes and pants.

Ten minutes later she joined him in the kitchen "Did you find out who Stefan was meeting?"

"Gossamer and Tully."

"What did they want?"

"They made another pitch for the water. Gossamer added something new to get him to come around."

"What?"

"Us."

"What do you mean?"

"Gossamer told him we were sleeping together. Your husband believed him. Told me he was going to kill me. That's what Gossamer wants. It would take two of us off the board. One in the ground, one on death row."

Grace winced. "Stefan wouldn't do that. He's incapable of it."

"Any man is capable of anything if provoked. He's crazy about you. He'd give up the water before he'd give you up."

She bit her lower lip. "What kind of proof does Gossamer say he has?"

"Stefan didn't say."

"Does Gossamer have anything else?"

Jack paused. "Like what?"

"I don't know."

"What are you hiding from me?"

Grace went to the sink and washed her hands. She dried them on a souvenir dish towel printed with a map of Tuscany. The names of towns were written in script. "Firenze. Siena. Monteriggione. San Gimignano." She kept her back to him.

Jack said, "Stefan told me he didn't care about your past when he met you. He said the old women down there spread all sorts of rumors about you and he didn't give a shit." He wound up and threw the changeup hard. "What did you do with our baby, Grace? What happened?"

Grace finished drying her hands and rehung the towel. She straightened it before turning toward him. Her lips parted as she breathed in, breathed out. He felt the doves fly by but no words came with them.

Deputy Santos was parked on a gravel road no wider than a tractor. Jack pulled off the highway and eased to a stop behind her patrol car. She unlocked the passenger door and he got in. The MDT screen bathed the front seat in a ghostly hue. Voices murmured over the two-way radio. A 12-gauge pump shotgun stood upright in its rack. The Smokey Bear hat lay on the seat between them.

"Been here long?" he asked.

"Not long. What brought you out here today?"

"The Fabros. It's what I told you before. Their water is at the center of this."

"They're not alone. I was able to compile a list. There are three others who've filed complaints."

"Let me guess. The cops didn't take them seriously because it sounded nothing worse than a pesky salesman sticking his shoe in the door. Did the complainants offer up any names or physical descriptions?"

"Two white males. One young. One with a beard."

"What's that narrow it down to, about seven million suspects?"

"More or less."

"Come up with anything else?"

"I checked the records and another three senior rights have changed ownership in the past six months but now the sellers are having trouble collecting. The buyer for each was listed as a different limited liability company."

"A shell within a shell within a shell. You can form an LLC online for fifty bucks," Jack said.

Deputy Santos said, "So I learned. I tried to chase them down, but the mailing addresses are care of a registered agent."

"The state requires an actual street address not a PO Box.

Registered agents provide one for a fee. It's all legal. What's happening with the arson investigation at your uncle's place?"

The radio squelched and a 911 dispatcher reported a domestic dispute in progress. The voice listed an address in a town at the other end of the county. Santos thumbed the volume down.

"The preliminary report calls it suspicious because the investigator found traces of a propellant in the hayloft. It'll take time to confirm because there were several different chemicals stored in the barn. Paint, diesel fuel, herbicides."

"What's your gut tell you?"

"Marco was murdered," she said flatly, but in the glow cast from the mobile display terminal's screen he could see the tightening at the corner of her eyes.

"Did you tell that to major crimes?"

"Not yet. I don't want to do anything that could be used to prejudice the arson investigation should it go to court."

"Good thinking. How long have you been a cop?"

"Five years, seven months. I was eligible for a training program after I got out of the army but I took a year off before enrolling when my partner became pregnant with the first of our two children. We have a boy and a girl."

"Afghanistan?"

"Iraq."

"Your partner a cop too?"

"No, she's a teacher. Middle school. The family joke is we're both in law enforcement. What about you, any kids?"

Jack thought on it, thought about Grace not saying a word. "Sort of." The deputy gave him a questioning look. "My wife and I are expecting."

"Blessings," she said. "So what did you find out?"

"There's an outfit in the city that's a hedge fund specializing in the wine trade. They don't advertise it but they're moving into water too. They seem pretty top heavy with private security guys. Being in Iraq, you'd recognize the type. I still need to check some things out."

"Meaning you're not ready to share names and specifics with me yet."

"No offense but I think it's like you holding off sharing everything with your major crimes folks. If I'm right, the top guy in all of this is politically connected. I don't want to make a legal mistake he could walk through."

The radio squelched again. This time 911 reported shots fired. Santos hit the volume but relaxed as soon as the location was given.

"There's one other thing." She tossed her head and the short pony tail bounced on her collar.

"Yeah, what's that?"

"I got a call from San Francisco PD. A Lieutenant Dolan."

Jack played it casual. "What did Terry want?"

"So you know each other."

"We go way back."

"There's a lot about you you haven't told me, isn't there?"

"We're on the same side here, Deputy. No matter what Terry said."

"Actually, he called about Grace Fabro. The name he used was Grace Millefiore."

"What did he say about her?"

"He said she may not be all she appears to be and asked if I had any information about her."

"What did you tell him?"

"I said as far as I know she's a law abiding citizen married to a member of one of the county's oldest and most upstanding families. Is there something else I should know?" She gave him a long look.

Hesitation prompted doubt, so Jack spoke right up. "Grace

and I go way back too. Before either one of us was married to other people. She asked me for help and I'm helping her. That's it. No matter what you may hear."

"Why should I hear anything else?"

"Because the people trying to get the Fabros' water are trying to get her husband to do something stupid that would clear the way for them. I know I'm asking you to go out on a limb trusting me but we're up against something that doesn't fall into any police procedural."

Santos stared out the windshield. The moon was up high and all the clouds had scattered. The mica in the crushed granite that graveled the road sparkled.

"When I was in Iraq it didn't take too long to figure out we hadn't been given it straight why we were there. The lies started from the very top and worked their way down the chain of command. Everyone knew it. Generals, captains, privates. We had our orders and we followed them. Most of the time it worked out all right but other times we had to do what we thought best, right then and there on the spot, not what the rules of engagement dictated." Deputy Santos took a breath. "You know what we called that?"

"I can guess."

"TRS. The real shit."

25

Dusk was settling over the city and Saints Peter and Paul Church glowed in a bright bath of well-positioned floodlights. The reflection from the white granite façade suffused Washington Square with a heavenly aura, the diocese hoping to offer its North Beach flock a holier alternative to the neon lure of nearby night clubs and strip joints. Wonder Boy was waiting on a park bench at the Stockton Street side of the square. He held a City Lights Bookstore bag on his lap.

Jack gestured at it when he arrived. "What did you buy, Ferlinghetti or Allen Ginsberg?"

"Neither. I collect biographies."

"Yeah, who?"

"People who s-s-share a s-s-similarity with Demosthenes. I bought one about S-s-sir Isaac Newton, another on Jimmy S-s-stewart."

"You never cease to amaze." Jack sat. "So why did you want to meet here? I take it there's something other than being up the street from a good bookstore."

"I found the post office box with no zip code. The one on the purple envelope."

Jack felt his stomach tighten. "Where is it?"

Wonder Boy pointed to a narrow building across the street that was wedged between a two-story flat and the San Francisco Italian Athletic Club. Three blue mailboxes were anchored curbside out front. The Stars and Stripes had already been lowered.

"It's one of the s-s-smallest post offices in the city but they s-s-still rent boxes inside."

Jack ran his tongue across his teeth. "And the name it's registered to?"

Wonder stared down at the books on his lap as if trying to draw strength from his fellow stutterers. "K Flowers," he said.

Jack didn't respond. His gaze turned from the dinky post office to Coit Tower that rose on the hill above.

"The initial *K*, not the name *K-a-y*," Wonder continued. "*K* as in one thousand as used in the metric s-s-system. As in a kilometer is one thousand meters. A *K* one thousand dollars."

"I get it, I get it." Jack took a deep breath. "Thanks for running it down."

He crossed over to the Filbert Steps and started climbing the 400 stairs to the white tower atop Telegraph Hill, drawn to the shining beacon like a moth to a flame.

COIT TOWER WASN'T a fancy lighthouse or an homage to Pisa. The money to build it came from a turn-of-the-century socialite named Lillie Hitchcock Coit who smoked cigars, gambled at North Beach men's clubs, and was a patron of San Francisco's volunteer fire department. The architects claimed the fluted shaft's resemblance to a fire hose nozzle was purely coincidental, but Jack's old man would thrust his hips and say the hell it wasn't a monument to his kind. "But it's a different sort of nozzle Firebelle Lil' be honoring, *boyo*."

To Jack, Coit Tower would always be a monument to first love. It was where he and Grace Millefiore rendezvoused when they started out. She'd grown up a few blocks away, and the park surrounding the shrine was both playground and refuge when she lived with her parents. Devout and old school, they fought hard to keep a tight rein on their beautiful daughter, but it was a lost cause. Grace started sneaking out at night when she was eleven. By thirteen she was picking pockets. When she turned twenty-one she'd already performed a dozen roles in sophisticated swindles, from ingénue to heiress to widow. She'd played a Spaniard, a Russian, and a Saudi princess in veils.

The first time Jack and Grace met there they sat on the top step and swigged Chianti from a green jug in a straw wrapper and ate salami and pecorino on pieces of warm bread they tore from a loaf of sourdough they'd bought at Molinari's. They talked about the music they liked, the food they liked, their favorite parts of the city, grifts they'd pulled, and grifts they wanted to pull. Jack tried to play it casual but he burned with desire from the get-go. When the wind picked up and she bunched her long raven hair in her fist and pressed it against her breast, he couldn't hold back any longer. He knocked over the bottle of Chianti as he grabbed for her, and it thumped down the concrete steps like the baby carriage scene in *Potemkin* while they kissed. It didn't break until it hit bottom.

From the tower's base he could see San Francisco spread out below and the towns and cities across the water. They formed a necklace of lights that circled the bay. But it wasn't a view Jack was after; he was looking for answers. There was no question who the little girl in the photograph was now, but the identity of the woman with her remained a mystery; so did the reason why

Grace hadn't told him about her and why she'd given the photos to Henri.

The wind picked up and carried with it the clanging of a cable car bell at the Taylor and Bay streets turnaround. The distinct tune was one of San Francisco's most joyous sounds, but Jack took no pleasure in hearing it. The idea that Grace had abandoned their daughter filled his mouth with bile. He knew he shouldn't be surprised that she'd done such a thing. Grace had always balked at being pinned down. She craved excitement, sought exotic locales, and thrived on assuming different guises for cons. The trouble was, Grace always struggled when it came time to leave a role behind. Jack used to caution her that she was in danger of losing her identity, and that to survive in the life, a grifter always needed to be able to return to their true self. It provided the only safe harbor in the dangerous world of make-believe. Shuffling skins so often took its toll on Grace when she and Jack were together, and her moods became like a game of poker with all wild cards and no limit. She could be cool under pressure one moment and then perilously intemperate the next. Strangely aloof and then wildly passionate.

Is that what drove her to ditch our daughter, Jack wondered? *Did she shed motherhood for a new role and lost her way back?* He saved the biggest question for last. *Could I've done more to save her?*

A minivan pulling into the parking lot snapped Jack back to the moment and he was glad for it. There was no going back in life, there were no do overs. A person bound by past mistakes was as good as a sitting duck. The minivan's occupants spilled out. Two kids raced each other up the steps while their parents trudged behind and issued warnings about being careful and not to push. The father hesitated as he passed by Jack.

"Would you mind taking our picture?" he asked.

"No problem," Jack said.

The family arranged themselves. The boy wore shorts and had a scrape on his knee. The girl had a barrette in her hair like the little girl in the photograph, the girl Jack would have to get used to thinking of as his flesh and blood. He moved down a couple of steps to get as much of the monument in the frame as possible.

As he was clicking the shutter, the father said, "Hey, tilt the camera so the tower leans like the one in Italy."

The family mugged as happy as fools, but Jack knew who the real fool on the hill was.

26

Terry and Katie were sitting at the dining room table. They both held cups of tea and the homicide cop looked as if he'd swallowed a spoonful of honey. When Katie turned around to greet Jack her cheeks were flushed.

"Terry was telling me this funny story. He was at a press conference with all the reporters and TV cameras crowding around him and this woman was there holding a baby—she was a witness or a relative of the victim, something like that, it doesn't matter—what does is, well, you tell it Terry. Tell Jack how the baby spit up. Tell him how it went all over your suit and you kept on talking as if nothing had happened. Guess what the photo caption said? 'Cop Keeps Cool in the Line of Fire.' Isn't that funny?"

Jack stared hard at Terry. "What the hell are you doing here?"

The honey turned to vinegar in the homicide cop's mouth. He set his cup down. Katie's smile somersaulted. "That's no way to treat friends," she said.

"Who said he is?"

"Don't do this. Please?"

Jack realized his fists were clenched.

Terry's eyes were locked on his. "Walk me down to my car so we can talk."

Jack glanced at Katie. The evening was going wrong when he needed it to go right. Before he could muster an apology she pushed away from the table. "You two can talk all you want. I'm going to bed."

Neither men moved as she left. When the door shut behind her, Terry said, "You don't deserve her."

"There you go again. You still think women are a prize you win for knocking down all the milk bottles. That's why I'm sharing a bedroom with her and you're not."

Terry's jaw hardened. "That go for Grace Millefiore too?"

"Why don't you ask her?"

"Maybe I will."

"Maybe you should've instead of peeping through keyholes first."

"What's that supposed to mean?"

"Your call to Deputy Florencia Santos."

Terry took a moment to register that. "You think you know everything but you're only fooling yourself. Just like you fooled Katie into believing you've changed. How are you going to be a responsible father when you can't even take responsibility for yourself?"

Jack didn't bother to count to three. "You better have a good reason for being here because it sure wasn't to lobby for godfather."

Terry ran his fingers down his rep tie even though it hung as straight as clock hands at six thirty. "What do you know about Jonathan Gossamer?"

"Took you long enough to take off the sommelier's gloves the brass are making you wear."

"Nobody tells me how to run an investigation."

"No? When you finally climb from cop to captain to chief they'll still be telling you who is above the law. It's the way it works. It's been that way ever since the Big Four cornered the railroads and divvied up all the land and built this town. Now it's tech not trains but we both know what's what."

"Answer the question."

Jack's gut told him the cop was in a trading mood and time to show a couple of cards. "Probably not much more than you've already found out. Gossamer's like countless other prospectors who've blown into San Francisco with the latest boom. He opened a bucket shop and started selling the wine industry to all the newly minted millionaires. Bet if you could get any of his investors to talk you'd find only the earliest ones have seen a payout. The rest are waiting for Godot."

"You mean it's a pyramid scheme."

"The shares aren't worth the papyrus they're written on."

"What's his connection to Grace Millefiore?"

Jack didn't flinch. "Happenstance. As Gossamer got deeper into his scam he realized the real money is in water, not wine, so he decided to add it to his portfolio of bogus investments. To salt the mine, he needed to show ownership of some senior water rights. Grace and Stefan Fabro fit the bill as a ready-made target."

"Do you have any proof or is that how you'd pull the same scam?"

"You asked, I answered."

Terry went to work adjusting the cuffs of his white shirt so they stuck out evenly from the sleeves of his navy blue suit jacket. Jack got ready for the curve ball.

"They're in it together," the cop said.

"You've lost me there. Who's in what together?"

"Gossamer and your girlfriend."

"Ex-girlfriend. Aren't you forgetting something? Grace and her husband are the victims. He's the one who was shot."

"You're half right. Stefan Fabro is the victim but he's also Grace's and Gossamer's mark. His family still has enormous landholdings."

"Better stick with homicides and leave solving scams to the fraud department."

"I have evidence."

"What kind?"

"I'm not at liberty to say."

Jack swung on instinct. "Let me guess. You had another go at Nurse Rainey. They finally spring her from the psych ward? She told you all about her affair with Jonathan Gossamer, that he was also sleeping with Alison, that he badgered her if she knew Grace and when she said she didn't, he dumped her. But that was all you needed, Grace and Jonathan Gossamer in the same sentence. What d'ya know, they must be working together." He jabbed a finger. "Other way around. Gossamer was targeting Grace. He knew she knew Henri LeConte, and so he was doing research to find something he could use as leverage to get her to hand over the water rights. Grifting 101."

Terry didn't say a word.

Jack swung again. "So after talking to Rainey you went and took another look at the boxes of fancy wine you found in the nurses' closets and guess what? You discovered they both included a bottle from Grace's vineyard."

The cop's hand went to his tie again and Jack knew he hit a double.

"That doesn't prove Grace guilty either. You might be able to link the wines to Gossamer but a bottle from the Fabro winery is circumstantial. You can buy it at a dozen shops in the city. My guess? Gossamer put it there on purpose. That's his hole card in case he needed more weight on her."

Terry left his tie alone. His face was a block of chiseled ice. "As I said, you think you know everything but you only know what you want to think."

"If you know everything why are you here?"

"I need truth not lies."

"Ask the question."

The former altar boy came as close to sneering as possible. "I don't care about some penny ante con game aimed at people smart enough to design a phone toy but too dumb to hold onto their money. What I do care about is Alison Kanasis. She's some-one's daughter, someone's sister. I want to catch her killer. And I care about Ji-min too. If she's still alive, I want to find her. If she's dead, I want to see her killer strapped to the chair in San Quentin's Green Room when the pellets drop."

"And you need my help."

"I need to get someone to talk right now because if Ji-min is still alive I can't wait for a jailhouse confession to rescue her."

"And who do you think that might be?"

"The same people who are running the con. They have a motive to kill Alison and make Ji-min disappear. The nurses can connect them."

"Aren't you forgetting a couple of things?

"What?"

"Opportunity and means."

"You saw the means. It was taped around Alison's neck. Opportunity? She was Henri LeConte's Monday nurse. The day he had his heart attack was the last day she worked for him and the last day anybody saw her alive. We've been able to track her from the minute she picked him up in Sausalito and crossed back over the Golden Gate."

"Her FasTrak. It logged the bridge toll."

"We also ran a search of citywide CCTVs. There are more than three thousand in the Financial District alone. We have her dropping LeConte off in front of a bank at the corner of California and Sansome. A couple of minutes later she's on tape entering a parking garage beneath the Pacific Tower building. They have a time stamp camera at the entrance to capture license plates in case people lose their ticket. It logged when she came in and when her car went out that night. Guess who has an office in that building?"

Of all the banks and all the parking garages in the city, Jack thought. *Maybe coincidences weren't only for Scientologists.* "You're reaching and you know it. Unless you got Gossamer behind the wheel of Alison's car or pulling a plastic bag over her head, you got nothing. And even if Gossamer is your man Grace had nothing to do with it."

"I have confirmation they work together."

"A bottle of wine is no proof."

"Maybe so but a report from Interpol that puts Gossamer and Grace together in Buenos Aires three years ago at the same time an Argentine cattle broker was scammed and wound up dead sure is."

The floor beneath Jack's feet yawed like the deck of a sailboat fighting through the Potato Patch.

Terry threw a lifeline. "There could be a way to keep her off death row."

Jack fought to keep his eyes fixed on the horizon. "What?"

"You convince Grace to roll on Gossamer. If she turns state's evidence and confesses now, she'll be able to cut a pretty good deal when it comes to sentencing. I doubt she'll get full immunity, but she won't take the fall for murder one. To make it work, she has to send Gossamer down."

The floor was still rolling and Jack had no choice but to roll right along with it.

~

KATIE WAS SITTING up in bed. She was reading her iPad with Chagall curled on the bed next to her. Jack went straight at it.

"I didn't mean to embarrass you but seeing Terry here, I got—"

She cut him off. "Jealousy is a vile cancer. First it attacks your self-confidence and reduces your ability to trust or love anyone. It corrupts all the good qualities that make you who you are. In the end you're left bitter and alone."

"I'm not jealous of Terry," Jack said quickly but held his temper. "I needed to do something and his being here kept me from doing it and I didn't want an excuse to keep from doing it."

Katie clutched the iPad to her chest. "What's so important you had to act like an ass?"

"I found something out tonight. Well, I had it confirmed. I've known it for a while but I'd convinced myself it wasn't true."

"Our marriage isn't a TV game show. Don't make me guess."

"It's something I need you to know because it's something about me and it's also something about us."

"Well, here I am. Tell away." Her face was a blank slate but her tone was easy to read.

"Those photographs of Henri's I told you about, the ones of a mother and child? They have nothing to do with him. They have to do with Grace. They have to do with me too. I don't know who the woman is but the child, she's Grace's. She's mine. Ours. From when we were together. There was a baby. I didn't know Grace was pregnant when we split up."

When Katie didn't respond he said, "What's that line from the movie? 'How do you con a con? Look in the mirror.' "

Katie didn't cry or get mad or accuse him. She said quietly, "What I was saying about jealousy? I wasn't referring to you. I was talking about myself."

And then she held up the iPad so Jack could see the screen. She had found the purple envelope and scanned the three photos and downloaded them into a slide show that also included snapshots of Jack and his brothers and sister when they were kids. There was a photo of his mother and father too. An image showed for a couple of seconds and then dissolved into the next. The slide show played over and over again.

"I knew it the moment I saw the pictures," Katie said. "She has Grace's blue eyes but the look in them and the expression on her face is all you. See how she holds her mouth, the way her brow knits? There's so much being said there. See the resemblance between her and the rest of your family?"

Jack felt the floor yaw again but in a different way this time.

Katie said, "What's her name?"

"I don't know." His head dipped. "I have a daughter and I don't even know her name."

"Do you know where she is?"

Jack shrugged.

"Well then," Katie said. "Seems you got your work cut out for you, cowboy."

27

Z-Pak's tongue was so swollen his mouth wouldn't close. Dark circles ringed his eyes and his skin was the color of a traffic safety cone. Jack was pretty sure he'd glow like a psychedelic poster if held under a black light.

"You don't look well," Jack said.

They were standing inside the parking garage at his building. Z-Pak had staked out the Citroën.

"Because of that scorpion. I'm allergic." His words were thick and slurred.

"If you want your gun back, you've wasted a trip. It's swimming with the fishes."

"Tully sent me. Mr. Gossamer wants to see you."

"Tell him to use Evite. Now get off my car."

"He means right now. Mr. Gossamer wants to make you a proposition."

"Have him try the Tenderloin. There's plenty who work the street corners down there."

Jack shouldered past him. Z-Pak yanked a snub nose from his jacket pocket and scuttled beyond reach. "Tully said don't take no for an answer."

"Ah, they gave you another gun. Isn't that sweet. What are you going to do, shoot me? Fail another mission for Tully and a dead scorpion will be the least of your problems."

Z-Pak looked down at the gun. Jack could all but hear the gears grinding in his antibiotic-riddled brain.

"I'll make it simple for you. Where does Gossamer want to meet?"

"There's a place on Geary. The Knight's Arms."

It was the bar Hark had gone to when he needed to gather intel on Tully. Jack said, "I'll be there at midnight."

"Tully said now."

Jack opened the car door and fired the ignition. He rolled down the window. "Midnight. And one other thing."

Z-Pak was still holding the revolver but it's two-inch barrel drooped. "What?"

He dropped a Jackson out the window. "Buy yourself some calamine lotion. You make me itch."

Jack's plan to drive to Clemens and confront Grace about their daughter went out the window too. As soon as he pulled out of the garage he got on the horn to Hark.

"What's up, *vato*?" the big man answered.

Jack filled him in. "The timing's not perfect but it is what it is."

"They won't try anything heavy in the bar," Hark said. "Everybody in that place carries and some of the dudes might side with us seeing we're the underdogs, we being two and they being three."

"Might?"

"There's always somebody who won't side with the outnumbered team no matter what. I could round up some *hermanos* to meet us there but then we'd outnumber Tully and company and they'd be the underdogs and then we'd be on the wrong side of the dudes who count noses and even the odds. You understand?"

"My guess it won't come to anything more than a I'll show you mine if you show me yours."

"What do they want to see?"

"The info Do Pray planted in the State's water database? The tracker pinged. Gossamer's taken a look-see. Either he bought the blue pearl wholesale or he still needs some convincing."

"And what are they going show?"

"It'll have to do with Ji-min and my Louisville slugger."

"The missing nurse." Hark whistled. "How you plan on playing that?"

Jack was cutting through the lower Mission. Windblown litter that could've been mistaken for large rodents skittered across the streets. "Terry's been watching too much TV if he thinks Grace is going to confess or get Gossamer to do the same. The punk will be sure to have plenty of deniability on his end whatever he chooses to reveal. But maybe he'll let something slip that will give us a bead on Ji-min and my bat."

"Where are you now?"

"Five minutes away. I'll pick you up."

"Let's take my whip. It's already got my bag of hardware in the trunk in case you're wrong about everybody only wanting to talk. It comes down to it and you got to grab something from there, remember I never keep an empty round in the chamber. One of the first things I learned on patrol."

THE ONLY CIVILIANS whoever stumbled into The Knight's Arms did so while playing Pokémon GO. A battle-scarred American flag hung on one wall. Another wall was festooned with regiment and unit colors. The music was loud and headbanging.

Bud was the beer of choice. Jack Daniels was drunk neat. The last person who ordered it mixed with a Coke lost his pants; they were hanging from the ceiling.

Hark led the way. He grunted "Hooah" to a table of bearded guys wearing desert digies and checkered keffiyehs around their necks. A line of quarters on the foot rail of the pool table was four dollars long. A third of the cues in the rack were broken in half. The bartender had a mohawk. 'The Right to Bear Arms' was tattooed on his left forearm. The right was a titanium prosthetic.

Tully and Z-Pak sat at a table with the wall at their backs. Z-Pak was jittery. Tully was not. He took in Hark and Jack without blinking.

Hark said, "I remember you from over there."

"No you don't." Tully said it as if he wasn't used to being questioned.

"It was at Bagram. You were the dude who stole a herd of goats. Your unit was going have a barbecue. A local sheik demanded them back. When you refused, the base commander ordered you to. Conducting public relations with the natives, he called it. So you said, okay, you'd deliver them personally. You loaded them onto a chopper, had the pilot circle over the sheik's village, and chucked them out. One by one."

Z-Pak giggled. Tully's stare at Hark was black. "Sounds like a story they tell FNGs to see if they can handle the truth."

"Only I was no fuckin' new guy. I was on my second tour. B Company. Forward operating battalion. What you got against goats?"

Tully's eyelids became slits.

Jack said, "I understand Gossamer wants to talk. Where is he, in the can?"

Tully said, "He'll be here when he gets here."

Jack cocked his head at Hark. "A regular existentialist, isn't he?"

Hark grinned. "John Paul Camus and Ringo too."

They took seats opposite. Z-Pak scratched at his face as he tipped his chair back and forth. A shot glass of amber liquid sat in front of Tully. It appeared untouched.

"That Irish whisky?" Jack said.

"What's it to you?" Tully said.

"Your name. I figure it's short for Tullamore Dew. That's cute, don't you know?"

"You're not funny," Tully said.

"I'm also not patient." Jack leaned forward. "Tell your boss I left. Tell him the water deal went with me."

He pushed out of the chair. Tully reached under the table. Hark moved fast for a big man. His Beretta M9 was out from under the tails of his untucked flannel in a blue flash and leveled at Tully's nose. Tully still didn't blink.

"I'll make the call," he said and held up a phone.

28

The waves were cracking hard against the rocks at Lands End and the night air was laden with salt. The lock on the metal gate at the upper parking lot had been cut. A black Lincoln crossover was backed into a stall closest to a memorial built to honor the USS San Francisco, a heavy cruiser that survived Pearl Harbor and saw action at Guadalcanal. The Lincoln's running lights were on but not the interior dome. Z-Pak's jacked up pickup was idling a few stalls away but with all its lights turned off.

Hark eased the '64 Chevy Impala past the open gate but stopped before going any further. Blue dash lights cast his face in an eerie glow.

"This reminds me of driving through the Korengal. We go in nuts to butts and sure enough, they pop up on the roof tops, our hummers and strikers like those little metal targets at a shooting gallery. The pings came so fast, so loud, my fillings hurt."

He turned to Jack. "You ever been hit by a .22?"

"That your way of saying someone's hiding in the trees like at Grace's winery?"

"Count on it."

Jack sucked his teeth. "You could throw it in reverse and we could call it a night."

"And miss all the fun?"

Hark planted his left foot firmly on the brake pedal and then stomped on the gas with his right. The V8 roared and the Flowmasters barked and the twin chrome tailpipes shot flames. The rear tires smoked as they spun in place and then he let off the brake. The lowrider shot straight at the Lincoln, closing the gap fast. At the last moment he stomped on the brakes with both feet and brought the Chevy fishtailing to a stop inches from the crossover's front grill.

"Hope they're wearing their brown pants," Jack said.

Tully burst from the Lincoln's driver's side door. "I ought to put a full clip through your windshield. Now back it up."

Hark had his window rolled down and pointed a middle finger at the cliff that dropped down to the cold waters of the Pacific below. "You first."

Jack said, "Good to know he has a temper. We can use that. Okay, time to conduct PR with the natives."

Hark said, "Just so you know, I hear a .22 ping, I'm going to bulldoze 'em right over the side. They'll drop like goats."

The Lincoln's dome light turned on. Jonathan Gossamer got out from the back seat. He was wearing a puffy down jacket. It was the same color as his shoes.

"Good evening. Or should I say good morning." He shivered and stuffed his hands deep into the jacket's pockets.

"Would've been warmer if you'd come down to The Knight's Arms a couple hours ago." Jack paused as if gathering his thoughts. "But then somebody would've seen you with us."

"Sometimes bravado has its place," Gossamer said. "This is not one of them."

"Z-Pak hiding in the woods or is he crouched in the back of his pickup?"

Gossamer smiled. "Who says he is the only one?"

"Who says we are? This is our town, remember?"

The smile slid off Gossamer's face. Tully's head swiveled as he started scanning the trees.

Jack said to Gossamer, "You called for the meeting. What do you want?"

Gossamer hunched his shoulders as if hugging himself. "Your sales pitch about selling water, perhaps I was too hasty in dismissing it. My people conducted some research and there may be something to the effect El Niño may have on groundwater basins that were overlooked during the drought."

"There's something to it, all right. The trick is knowing which basins."

Gossamer bobbed. He was either nodding in agreement or trying to keep his teeth from chattering. "It is too late and it is much too chilly to stand out here braving the elements while we play games, Mr. McCoul. I am inclined to cut to the proverbial chase."

"By all means, cut away."

"Your reputation is not lost on me. Far from it. I am actually somewhat of an admirer of your early work. Given the historical context in which you operated, you were quite a trail blazer. But times have changed and so have the methods. There is a much higher degree of sophistication required now, would not you agree?"

"If we're cutting to the chase, why don't you cut straight to the part about how much money you're going to pay me for the name of the groundwater basin filled with H2O and how you can get your hands on it."

Gossamer's teeth gleamed. "I was speaking of cutting to the chase about you and Grace Millefiore." He let it sit for a few moments. "I do enjoy hatching surprises. Yes, Grace's history is well-known to me too. As a matter of fact, our paths have crossed before. Serendipity, it would seem, brought us together again. At first I was inclined to believe her tale of leaving her old life behind but then I remembered no one is really ever free of their past nor truly innocent. It turns out I was proven correct and serendipity has turned into an opportunity. A golden opportunity."

He pulled his hands out of his pockets, clasped them together, and blew on them. His breath was the color of sea smoke. "Tell me I am wrong. Tell me you and Grace are not pulling a con and using the rather oblivious Mr. Fabro to assist you." He held his hands outstretched. "It is only equitable that I capitalize on my discovery, would not you agree?"

"I already offered to sell you a piece of the basin. If you don't want in, there are others."

"Oh, but I do I want in. However, I want some answers first." He licked his lips.

"I'm not going to tell you where it is."

"I already know that. Sabbia Plain."

Jack feigned shock. "How did you..."

Gossamer allowed himself a self-satisfied smile. "As I said, times have changed. So have methods. I also have a copy of the recorded deed when the property changed hands recently from the Fabros to a holding company. I am sure we can both agree the members of the LLC are Grace and you. What did she do, manipulate her husband into giving her Sabbia Plain as an anniversary gift?"

"So you did some digging. And maybe you think you know everything. But that doesn't mean you're entitled to a discount."

"A discount for what? A basin that is surely as dry as it always has been since the Pleistocene Age? I grant you, the records do look authentic upon first glance but, please, consider who you are trying to deceive."

"I don't know what you're talking about."

"Of course you do. Again, it is much too cold and damp out here to play games. I do congratulate you on the idea of selling a dry hole. So much so that I am prepared to take it off your hands and sell it myself."

Jack flashed surprise again and then said, "What will you give me for it?"

"Your life, of course." Gossamer snapped his fingers. Tully pulled out a phone, clicked an app, and handed it to Jack. "Even these inexpensive go phones come with cameras now. The quality is actually quite good."

Photographs filled the screen. They were shots of Ji-min with her head bashed in. Close-ups of her damaged skull, a pool of fresh blood. Shots of the Louisville slugger. Jack studied them as he scrolled.

Gossamer said, "Imagine what the police will think when they lift your fingerprints off the bat, your DNA too. Do you know how many cells a hand sloughs off every time it grips something? Amazing."

"I suppose killing her saves you from having to pay her a cut," Jack said. "She was working with you, right?"

Gossamer smirked.

Jack said to Tully, "Murdering a woman help bring back memories of your service days?"

Tully's eyes were bottomless pools as if the photographs were a list of box scores in the sports section.

Gossamer stuck his hands back in the pockets of his puffy jacket. "Give Mr. Tully back the phone. We have plenty of copies on other devices but we would not want you to harbor any illusions."

Jack considered hurling it. He was sure he could chuck it far enough to clear the USS San Francisco Memorial and the stand of trees between the parking lot and the edge of the cliff. Instead he took another look at every image before handing it over.

Gossamer's tongue flicked across his lips. "Transferring the deed to me will require both you and Grace's signatures. We will be in touch with a time and place. Good night, Mr. McCoul."

JACK BAGGED three hours of sleep. Katie woke him with a kiss on the lips and a double espresso.

He sat up. "Where are you going?"

She was wearing a faded denim jacket over a persimmon top and black cropped yoga pants. "It's a work day. We have a team meeting at the Bayview gym and then I'm leading an expectant mother's class in Oakland. Don't forget to walk Chagall. See you tonight."

Before he could tell her he was going to drive out to Grace's, she was gone. He started in on the espresso. The first gulp cleared the cobwebs. The second triggered the glimmering of a plan. By the time he was out of the shower and dressed, he had a strategy in place and a set of tactics to go with it.

That's when his phone buzzed. Jack was long past being surprised by anything.

"I'm downstairs," Grace said. "Buzz me in. We need to talk."

She met him on the landing. "I thought you'd never move out of the Mission District."

"South of the Slot suits me fine," he said.

"Because it's only a few blocks from the ballpark and halfway between The Pier Inn and Abuelita's." Grace tried a smile.

"You still like your macchiato with a sprinkle of clove on the foam?"

"Listen to us," she said.

Jack led the way into the loft. Chagall scrambled from the

bedroom and greeted her with a wagging stump. She scratched him behind the ears.

"I should have known you'd take care of him. I hear Henri's doing much better. Taylor told me he's able to stay awake for an hour or so at a time. He's still not able to move much or speak but she said that will come with physical and speech therapy."

Jack gave the espresso machine another workout. Grace explored the loft. She touched the shelf of mementos, surveyed the framed snapshots, ran her fingertips along the back of the couch. The windows drew her.

"Will you and Katie move to a bigger place after the baby's born?"

"Let's talk about the baby that's already been born. You bought her that silver barrette she's wearing when you visited Bolivia. That means you've seen her since you gave her up."

Grace kept staring out the window. The streets below were thick with truck traffic and a pair of tugs were hooking up a tanker moored at Anchorage Nine.

"It's why I'm here. I wanted to tell you I was pregnant when we were in Prague but I couldn't, and I've wanted to tell you ever since but I didn't know how. With all that's been happening, I—"

"Start with her name," Jack said.

"Zita. It means..."

"Little girl in Spanish."

"In Italian too."

"You name her that?"

"I would've named her Simone after my mother, but I wasn't in a position to fill out a birth certificate. The friend I left her with started calling her Zita. It stuck."

"Where is she?"

"On a remote *estancia* in Argentina. It's far away from everywhere."

"The place in the photographs. The ranch in the painting in

your office with the mountains behind it. Those are the Andes. Who's the woman with Zita?" The name came off his tongue as if he'd been saying it for years.

"A saint."

"You mean a nun?"

"No. I went into labor prematurely. This was in Buenos Aires. Catalina, that's my friend's name but she wasn't my friend then because I'd never met her before, was at the clinic too. She was visiting her niece. Anyway, I had the baby and Catalina came into my room by mistake. Or maybe it wasn't. Maybe it was divine intervention. I don't know."

Jack watched Grace's reflection in the glass as she spoke. For a moment he could see a younger version.

"I was pretty out of it," she said. "It was a very difficult delivery and when I woke up, Catalina was at my bedside. I imagined she was my mother, and I started talking to her and told her everything about my life and asked for forgiveness. How I had treated her as a daughter. What I had done. You, me, the baby. Everything. Catalina held my hand and kept patting it. It wasn't until later I realized she didn't speak English. But she understood me. She understood why I couldn't keep the baby. Why I had to leave the clinic right away. And so she agreed to care for her until I could. It was only going to be for a little while but one day turned into the next and then a week into a month and..." Grace choked up.

"You didn't think I should know? Didn't think to call me, that I'd be there as fast as a plane could take me?"

"I didn't know what to think. It was so hard to leave you in the first place. And then having the baby on my own."

"Did Gossamer call you last night and tell you to come talk to me or did he wait until this morning?"

Grace spun around. "What are you talking about? Why would he call me?"

"Because you were with him in Buenos Aires. Terry Dolan told me. Remember him? He's a homicide detective now. He got a report from Interpol about Buenos Aires. Gossamer confirmed he knew you when he put the squeeze on me last night. I figured his next call would be to you to make sure I didn't have second thoughts."

"Well, he didn't call me."

"Why should I believe you? You haven't been straight about this since the get-go."

"Gossamer really did find me by accident. I should've told you right off I knew him once upon a time, but then you would-n't've helped me."

"You didn't give me a chance?"

"Would you have given me one?"

Jack sucked his teeth and the heat of the moment passed. "Tell me about Buenos Aires."

Grace turned back to the window and took a deep breath. "Stupid. Stupid. Stupid. After everything I learned from Henri and you, I should've known better than to get involved with players I didn't know. What I told you, that I needed some time to figure everything out after Prague? It's true. I was staying at the Ritz-Carlton and Jonathan Gossamer tried to pick me up at the hotel restaurant one evening. I could see right through him and told him he'd targeted the wrong mark. He laughed it off and then told me about the con he was working on a cattle broker. It was a variation of the Iraqi dinar only with livestock from Uruguay. He said my pregnancy would work perfectly into the script—who wouldn't trust a pregnant woman? He agreed to pay me twenty percent of the score for what amounted to a walk-on."

"You had the whole take from Prague. Why did you agree to it?"

"I was worried I didn't have enough for a fresh start and the role he was offering was easy money. And then wouldn't you know it I went into labor the night before the deal was supposed to go down. I took a cab to a clinic and when I finally came to, I saw on TV the mark had been killed. Don't you see? I was afraid Gossamer would come after me because I could connect him to it, but I couldn't go to the police because I was in on the play. I had to get away but I couldn't take the baby with me because Gossamer would be searching for a woman with a newborn. Now do you understand why I had to give Zita up? It was to keep her safe."

"Why did you stay in Argentina?"

"I didn't know if the police were already on to me or how far Gossamer's reach went, what border officials he'd been able to get to. I hid out for a year. Later, I heard he was back in Switzerland."

"You could've gotten the baby then and come home to San Francisco but you didn't."

She pressed her forehead against the glass and her shoulders sagged.

Jack answered for her. "Because you met Stefan."

"I wasn't looking for love but it happened. And with it came a new life too."

"What you've always been looking for." Jack paused. "You could've told Stefan about Zita."

"I didn't know how without admitting to my past. I couldn't do that to him. And there was something else."

"What?"

She kept her forehead against the glass. "I didn't want Zita to learn about who I'd been either. What I'd done with my life, the things I did. Stealing. The cons. I was afraid she wouldn't love me. I was terrified she might turn out like me."

Jack went to the sink, turned the water on hot, and rinsed

out the cups. He knew she meant her turbulent streaks, her moods. "Stefan still doesn't know about her, does he?"

"No."

"But Gossamer does."

Her breath fogged the window. She drew a slash through it with the tip of her finger. "When he found me here and asked what happened I told him about going into labor. I told him the baby was stillborn and I was in a coma for months and nearly died. I made it sound like I didn't know anything about the mark's murder."

"But either he didn't believe you or he needed to make sure."

"Somehow he learned about the photos. He came back at me and threatened Zita if I didn't hand over the water rights."

Jack felt his fists clenched. "That's his real leverage on you. Winging Stefan was to let you know he was serious. Why didn't you tell me about all this when you first asked for my help?"

"I... I didn't want you to think I'm a bad mother because I put our daughter's life at risk."

Jack's blood stirred at hearing *our*. "Maybe he's bluffing about knowing where she is."

"He's not. I called Catalina. She says she's seen strange men in the little village near the *estancia*. They've taken up residence above the bodega."

"And now he wants Sabbia Plain too."

"Once he gets it he's going to kill me because what I know about Buenos Aires and he'll have his hired thugs kill Zita too."

"That's not going to happen," Jack said.

"How can we stop him?"

"Play out the blue pearl like we planned. Spring a trap that will put him behind bars forever. He's responsible for two deaths already."

Thought lines furrowed Grace's forehead. "If luring you to

Henri's houseboat was a setup, the nurse is probably in on it too. Those photos he showed must have been staged."

"Ji-min's in on it all right. She has been from the beginning. They may have faked her death, but that doesn't mean Gossamer still won't kill her if he needs to make his leverage stick."

"But you have a plan to keep that from happening, don't you?"

"That I do."

29

"You mean you got two baby mamas and you're only telling me now?" Hark's tone said it all.

Jack said, "I'm still getting my head around it myself."

"But *vato* you know if it comes down to it I got to back Katie. All due respect."

They were in Katie's Prius having switched the Citroën for it. The plain vanilla car made tailing Z-Pak easier.

"It's not going to." Jack let a car get between them and the jacked-up pickup. They were on Fourth Street heading away from downtown. "This is about keeping Zita safe."

"I like that name. Have a little cousin called that. She's a chile pepper, all right. Run it by me again how this *pendejo* got hold of Henri's photos?"

Jack told him about Gossamer confronting Grace at the vineyard. Right after that she sent the photos to Henri.

"For insurance in case he didn't believe her, which he didn't," Hark said. "She knowing Henri would give them to you in case things went south."

"Gossamer's one of those pigs in the forest that can smell

truffles," Jack said. "He did some homework and found out about Henri and Grace's history and used the nurses to root out any secrets. Alison must have seen the snapshots and told Gossamer. She didn't mean any harm because she didn't know what they were. Henri being Henri got a sixth sense that something was up so he took them to the bank for safekeeping. The effort getting there was too much for his heart."

"Bad luck all the way around. It happens." Hark paused as he eyed a motor scooter zipping in and out of traffic. "Still, I don't make Goss for killing the nurse. You said Terry told you they had no witnesses of anyone going in or going out of her apartment. That takes a special talent to pull that off. And a plastic bag taped around the neck? They teach that in the same school as waterboarding."

"Meaning Tully."

"He's got the résumé for it, just saying."

They passed the train station and crossed over China Basin. Up ahead Z-Pak merged onto Third Street and threaded his way through the new Mission Bay medical complex. Jack held the Prius three car lengths back.

Hark said, "He's probably got a crib in Dogpatch. When we go in there, we better be as quiet as Tully if we don't want the police coming down on our ass."

"You know I'm going to bring Terry in on this eventually."

"Fine by me as long as eventually is not right now. Look. He's turning."

They made the turn too but kept on going when Z-Pak made a quick left. Jack circled around the block in time to see the pickup pull into the driveway of a squat cinder block building. He got out, unlocked a sagging chain link fence, drove the truck in, parked, and closed and relocked the gate.

"What do you think?" Jack said.

"If you wanted to stage a make-believe killing, that'd be the place. But you know she may not be alive no matter what you saw on that phone."

"Her little finger. It was curled in one shot and not in the other."

"That was then. This is now. She could be in there dead for real."

"One way to find out. You ready?"

"When wasn't I?"

Jack parked and they walked down the sidewalk. The street was only a few blocks long. Half the buildings were light industrial, the other half older flats that reflected the neighborhood's gritty working-class history. Newer buildings were sprouting up on surrounding blocks as redevelopment oozed from downtown.

"How would Tully play it?" Jack asked as they arrived at the chain link gate.

"He'd sneak in at night wearing NV goggles."

"You got any of those?"

Hark patted his pockets. "Damn. Must've left 'em at home."

Jack grabbed the top of the gate and scrambled over.

Hark followed. "So much for sneaking in, sneaking out."

Jack pounded on the door. "PG&E. We need to check your pilot light."

The door cracked opened. "Huh? Wait a minute, you're not PG&E guys."

Jack pushed through. Hark was right behind him. "You pull another gun on me you're going in the shark tank."

Z-Pak's skin was scratched raw in spots. "How did you get here?"

"Where's Ji-min?" Jack said.

"Who's that?"

Hark was already opening doors and drawers. It didn't take long to search the place. The building was the size of a double-car garage and reeked of pesticides. A sink and stove were in the corner. A cot with a sleeping bag served as a bedroom.

"No one here. Found this under his pillow." He held out the snub-nosed revolver. "Dude lives pretty clean. He's the only roach in the place."

Z-Pak shuddered. "What do you want?"

"To simplify things," Jack said. "You're going away."

"Why me?"

"Throwing a Molotov at the Fabros for starters. Torching their neighbor's barn with a kid in it."

"What kid? I don't know about no kid."

"Try reading the news. The cops might chalk it up as manslaughter to go along with arson but then there's the nurse." Jack shook his head sympathetically. "That'll put you on death row."

Z-Park worked his fingernails into his cheek. "I had nothing to do with that. I wasn't even there."

"There being where, the parking garage?"

"She pulled in right when Tully and Mr. Gossamer were getting out of the car. She started screaming at Mr. Gossamer. Called him all sorts of names. Two-timer. Shit like that."

"See, that's where you're making a mistake. If you weren't there like you say, then how do you know what she said?" Jack waited. It came easier than he'd hoped.

"Tully told me later. She was throwing such a fit the had to quiet her down. Then he stuck her in the trunk. He texted me to come give him a ride after he drove her back to her apartment in her car and left her there. So you see I didn't have nothing to do with it."

Jack raised his palms. "But then there's the other nurse. Ji-min. I saw the photos. Somebody used my bat on her."

Z-Pak went to work raking the other cheek. "Wasn't me. Besides her name's Carol. And she's not dead neither."

Hark was standing behind him. "Good one, spotting the curled finger."

Jack closed in on Z-Pak even though his ravaged face repulsed him. "Two choices here."

"What are they?"

"Tell us where Ji-min, er Carol, is."

"What's my other choice?"

"You don't want to know."

Hark hissed and made a rattling sound behind him.

"Okay, okay. She's staying with Mr. Gossamer."

"Where is she from?"

"I don't know. Europe or some country like that. Mr. Gossamer and her are old friends. He called her in for help. Had her dress up like a nurse."

"She plays dead pretty good. She do her own makeup for the photos?"

Z-Pak was scratching his cheeks with both hands. "Maybe. I don't know. I guess. She always looks different. Last time I saw her she was a blonde."

"My bat at Gossamer's too?"

"Maybe. I don't know. I guess. Why?"

Jack gave a let's-wrap-it-up twirl of the fingers to Hark.

Z-Pak shifted nervously. "What about me? I told you what you wanted."

"First, give me your phone."

"Okay so long as you don't surf the net. I got a limited data plan. You'll give it back, won't you?"

"Second, give Hark the keys to your truck. You're going for a ride."

"Where to?"

"The jail in Clemens."

"Wait a minute. Now wait a minute. That's not what we agreed."

"We didn't agree on anything."

"Sure we did. I took the first choice. I did. You heard me. I told you what you wanted. We had a deal."

"We did and going to jail is part of it."

"That sucks. Don't I get to call a lawyer or something?"

"You can ask the deputy when you get there, but something tells me she may not be in too understanding of a mood. The barn you burned down? That was her uncle's. And the kid inside? Her cousin."

30

Jack kept an eye out for opossums as he negotiated an alley between a cluster of luxury towers. A light drizzle fell and droplets were beading on the bill of his Giants cap. Trash cans clanged at the back door of a Chinese restaurant as kitchen workers called it a night. A shadowy figure lurked in a doorway up ahead. When Jack approached a man stepped out.

"Here's the s-s-security pass," Wonder Boy said.

Jack slid it into his pocket. "Thanks."

"It provides entrance to the underground parking garage. There's a bank of elevators there. One is marked S-s-service. Gossamer is on the twenty-s-s-second floor. Number 223. There are only thirty floors. Each has four units except for the top four floors. Those are penthouses."

"Pretty exclusive neighborhood with few neighbors."

"One hundred s-s-sixteen units total but most are owned as parking lots for foreign money. The tower is less than a third occupied full-time."

"This will open Gossamer's unit too?"

"It's a master copy s-s-so it s-s-should even if he's altered the lock code. Anything else?"

"As long as Gossamer believes a fire alarm going off at one in the morning is something you don't question, I'm good."

"You're s-s-sure he's there?"

"Do Pray hacked into the building's CCTV system. He has footage of Gossamer and a woman with blond hair getting off the elevator and entering the apartment a couple of hours ago. That's got to be Ji-min or Carol or whatever she calls herself. There's no sign they've left."

"What about the other two men?"

"Z-Pak's under wraps. I'm not certain about Tully but I'm betting he's up there with Gossamer. That's what he gets paid for."

"Does the s-s-security tape s-s-show it?"

"It has him driving into the garage and letting Gossamer and the woman out in front of the elevator. They went up and Tully drove off to park. He's a trained ghost. He knows where the camera blind spots are and instinctively stays inside them."

"The s-s-statistical odds of him being in the apartment are fifty-one percent when I factor in biological needs, personal habits, and random events."

"I'll take my chances."

"There is only a forty-two percent chance you'll s-s-succeed."

"That high? Here, I got something for you." Jack reached in the duffle bag hanging from his shoulder and pulled out a package. "It's a bio on John Lee Hooker."

Wonder held it reverently. "His s-s-song 'S-s-stuttering Blues' is an anthem."

~

JACK FOUND the service elevator and placed the electronic security pass against the reader. A green light flashed and the doors opened. He pushed the button to twenty-three.

The elevator didn't stop at any other floors. The doors opened at twenty-three. He stuck his head out and located the alarm panel connected to the floor's photoelectric heat and smoke detectors. It was conveniently placed right across the hall from the service elevator. He pushed twenty-one and rode down two flights. The floor had the same layout. He hit the emergency stop and crossed to the alarm control panel. Rows of indicator lights showed that all the photoelectric heat and smoke detectors on the floor were functioning properly. His father hadn't given him much in life other than a hard time but he did pass on an understanding of how firefighting equipment worked. Jack opened the panel and tripped the sensors to the apartment right below Gossamer's. That triggered the alarm. A siren wailed and a computerized voice blared directing residents to evacuate immediately.

Jack stepped back into the elevator car and lifted the emergency phone. "We got smoke on 21. Oh shit, I can see flames. I'm out of here."

He pushed the ground floor button and jumped back out before the doors closed. He sprinted to the emergency exit, raced up to floor twenty-three, and waited in the stairwell. No one came down. It would be a few minutes before people took the evacuation seriously. He knew when they did most would descend by elevator rather than take the stairs as instructed. The higher the rent, the costlier the mortgage, the more likely residents rode not walked.

Five minutes later his phone buzzed. "I got y'all's people on the monitor," Do Pray said. "They took the elevator and are standing on the street out front."

"Two men and a woman?"

"Naw. Only the man and woman I seen going in a couple hours ago. Still no sign of the driver. Maybe he left the car and went out clubbing or something."

The chance of success dropped by half but Jack had no choice. "Keep an eye on them and shoot me a text if they head for the elevator or if you spot Tully."

He walked down a flight. The hallway on twenty-two was empty. The noise from the alarm was deafening, the grating computerized voice constant. He went to 223 but didn't put his ear to the door. Luxury buildings featured ample soundproofing and if Tully was inside he'd be as silent as a knife.

Jack slipped on latex gloves. The security pass unlocked the door. He twisted the knob. No one was waiting in the entryway. He began a quick check. The floor plan was open. An island separated the living room and kitchen. Two bedrooms and adjoining bathrooms were down a hall. The furnishings throughout had the personality of a business hotel. He checked the master bedroom first. He looked under the bed and opened the closet. Six identical pairs of red Pumas were in a shoe rack. The clothes were all the same size. His thirty-two-inch red and black alloy slugger baseball bat wasn't hidden there. He unslung the duffle bag and pulled out the bat's twin. He held it by the barrel and stuck the butt into one of the shoes and gave it a few twists and then pushed the grip inside the sleeve of one of the blazers for good measure.

He carried the bat to the second bedroom. The closet held a mix of designer dresses, conservative pant suits, and high heels. He entered the bathroom. The makeup in the bathroom was plentiful and expensive. He picked up a hair brush and ran the soft bristles up and down the bat's barrel and gave it a swipe with a mascara wand.

There was no sign of a second man living in the apartment. Jack returned to the living room and looked out the windows. Red lights flashed from a fire engine and a hook and ladder below. His phone buzzed with an incoming text.

Spotted Tully on 18. Taking stairs up.

Jack sped up his search. He checked every closet, looked under the couch, opened the pantry. He found his bat hidden behind a stacked washer and dryer in the utility room. He replaced the alloy slugger with the doctored twin. His phone buzzed with another text.

Split. Now.

Jack threw open the front door and waved the security pass at the door straight across the hall as the door to the emergency exit at the end of the hall started to open. The light blinked green, the lock clicked, and he straight-armed his way in and pulled it shut behind him. He yanked out a hair and placed it in front of the bottom jam and then moved to the side and held his breath.

Tully was standing on the other side of the door. Jack could sense him. He pictured a gun aimed center mass. The door handle jiggled then stopped. Jack counted to sixty as he kept his eyes on the loose hair. Finally it twitched, sucked by the draft from the door across the hall opening and closing. Jack let his breath out slowly. He gave it another minute before checking. The hallway was empty.

He was through the emergency exit, down twenty-two flights of stairs, and out through the parking garage to the alley in two minutes flat. He peeled off the gloves and dropped them in the Chinese restaurant's trash can. His pulse slowed as he stuck to the buildings and headed back to his loft. He didn't make it three blocks before a black Crown Vic pulled alongside. The window rolled down.

"Not one of the city's most scenic routes for a midnight stroll," Terry Dolan said.

Jack broke stride. "Taking advantage of the city's liberal overtime rules?"

"What were you doing inside Gossamer's building?"

"He live in that tower with the alarms going off? What d'ya know? I was passing by and looked in to see if I could lend a hand in case anyone needed help rescuing a cat."

"Can it. My guys made you going in and coming out."

"How long have you had it staked out?"

"No comment."

"That long, huh? My advice? Talk to a judge about getting a search warrant for Gossamer's apartment."

"You were up there?"

"No comment."

The homicide cop was twisted in his seat. He didn't seem to care it was putting a wrinkle in his white shirt. His Adam's apple mimicked an elevator. Jack knew he was swallowing his pride.

"What would I find up there?"

"By the time you get the warrant I'll let you know."

"I need more of an answer."

"It'll have to do for now. We done here?"

"What's in the bag?"

"Workout clothes. I was at one of Katie's gyms. She has me leading one of her classes now. Weight lifting for expectant fathers."

Terry drummed the steering wheel. "I could arrest you for pulling a fire alarm without cause. Run you down to the Hall and lock you up. Give you some time to think about telling me what you're not telling me."

"Even if you had proof, think how it'd look: San Francisco's top homicide detective misses solving a murder because he was making a misdemeanor collar. Not exactly a career builder. So much for becoming a captain. Better if you keep your eyes peeled on your inbox."

"And what would I be expecting?"

"Something other than a birth announcement, don't you know?"

31

A whorl of blackbirds undulated across the early morning sky. The feathered cloud was as untethered as a tumbleweed bouncing along the hardpan. The water that filled the canal below nearly reached the top of its concrete embankments, but the aqueous ribbon's movement was impossible to detect. No wavelets lapped, rapids babbled, or falls roared.

Jack tried reading the water for signs. The flow contained more than atoms and molecules. Water carried the past as well as the future, from ancient rains to the promise of new life. The aqueduct linked California's north and south but the water in it was part of all the water on Earth. Clouds born over oceans broke on mountaintops and the water ran downhill to return to the sea. Powerful currents mixed it all together and distributed it across the globe to form new clouds that broke someplace else. Jack looked down the length of the canal to where it disappeared from view. Part of him existed beyond the horizon too. Like water, strands of his DNA—its atoms and molecules—had mixed with Grace's and were now flowing in a three-year-old child.

A white and green patrol car pulled up behind the Citroën parked alongside the highway by the Clemens bridge. Deputy Florencia Santos put on her Smokey Bear hat, hitched up her utility belt, and joined him.

"I hope you're not going for a morning dip," she said. "You'd be surprised how many people treat the canal as a swimming pool."

"I'll keep that in mind next time I drink from the tap."

The broad brim cast a half-moon shadow on the deputy's face. "The man your friend Hark brought me won't shut up. He screamed all night that his cell was crawling with insects. He's no different than a junkie going cold turkey. Scratching his skin and wetting himself."

"Z-Pak confess to burning down your uncle's barn yet?" Jack asked.

The deputy's hat bobbed. "He's told me more than I care to hear. When he was a kid, his uncle molested him and gave him a magnifying glass to keep quiet. He discovered if he held it over a bug in the sunlight it would catch on fire. A stint in juvenile hall didn't turn him into a Boy Scout any. Somewhere along the line he became convinced all those bugs he burned up were out to get him."

"Doesn't sound like they prevented him from lighting any more fires."

"He swears he was only following orders when it came to the barn and wine cellar. He wouldn't tell me who issued them but you're going to."

"I take it you haven't charged him yet."

"There's still time on the twenty-four hour hold until I have to or let him go. Before the clock runs all the way down, how about you tell me what's really going on here."

Jack dipped both hands in the canal. The water was cold. He splashed his face and watched the droplets fall back into the canal. He wondered how long it would take for them to become clouds over the Andes and then fill a bath used by his daughter.

"It's like this," he began and laid it out for her.

"Nailing Gossamer for pulling a con isn't good enough," Jack said. "He'd just bond out and disappear. Guys like him shed their identities as easy as snakes and show up someplace else to do it all over again. Same with his muscle, Tully. The army trained him in evasion. He'd melt into the night and be on a plane to the Mid-East or Africa or wherever there's a despot willing to pay him."

The deputy's lips formed a frown. "I met a couple like him. That kind was never motivated by love of country."

"To stop them they got to go down for murdering the nurse."

"If they step foot in my county again, I'll put the zip ties around their wrists myself."

"I know you would, but it'll be a whole lot cleaner if Terry Dolan is the one to charge them since killing Alison happened in his jurisdiction. Tully did it but Gossamer as good as taped the bag around her neck himself."

The deputy thought it over. "What about my cousin? They're both accessories to Marco's death."

"The only witness who can prove that is Z-Pak. A judge might be willing to make a deal to get him to testify against them if it has the dead nurse as part of it. Killing her should be enough to put Tully and Gossamer away for good, and Z-Pak can take the weight for the arson and Marco."

The deputy thought some more. "You'd like it if I waited to charge him until the other two are behind bars, is that it?"

"If they get wind he's in jail they'll book."

"How are you going to keep them from finding out?"

Jack held up Z-Pak's phone. "They text, don't talk."

The deputy said, "I'll give Lieutenant Dolan a call so we can coordinate the arrests."

"Okay but something has to happen first and the timing is tricky."

He could feel her gaze from under the hat brim bearing down on him. "What kind of thing?"

"An exchange of leverage."

"Is Dolan party to this?"

Jack gave a noncommittal shrug. "As much as he officially can be. Same for you, if you get my drift."

She reached up and squared her hat even though it didn't need squaring and hitched her utility belt even though it didn't hitching. "This so-called exchange better be over in eight hours because that's when I'm going to charge Z-Pak with murder. No way I'm letting my cousin's killer walk."

"It will be," Jack said.

⁓

HARK WAS SITTING on the porch swing watching Eddie and Chaco play dominoes.

"Where did you stash Z-Pak's truck?" Jack asked.

Hark hooked a thumb at an outbuilding. "There's a tractor in there too. I told Grace I could give it some styling, she wants. Switch out the exhaust and spark arrestor for chrome pipes, lay some flames down on the cowling. Pinstripes at least."

"You guys ready to ride?" Jack asked.

Eddie and Chaco thumped their chests with their fists.

Hark said, "That mean Goss and Tully confirmed when and where?"

"They did. I'm going to tell Grace now."

She was in the kitchen making sandwiches. A pot of *pappa al pomodoro* simmered on the stove and the steam from the soup carried wafts of tomatoes, garlic, and basil with it.

"Hark told me he wants to cherry your tractor," Jack said.

"His way of an olive branch." She smiled. "You told him about Zita."

"Have you told Stefan yet?"

Her attention went back to the sandwich makings. "I will but not right now. Maybe after we're clear of all this. It'll be easier then."

"Where is he?"

"Working in the office. Despite everything that's going on, this is still a business that needs running. Supplies have to be ordered, field hands hired. Spring won't wait. The harvest either. Being off schedule a couple of days can ruin a vintage."

"You really are into this. Winemaking, cooking, the country life. The whole deal."

"I am but this mess with Gossamer is a cloud I can't seem to get out from under. I know I'm to blame."

"Let's grab some air," he said.

She put the assembled sandwiches on a platter and covered them with a fresh dish towel. They took the backdoor into the vineyard. The sky showed some blue. The sun was a pale yolk.

Jack told her about the message from Gossamer and the timing of the meet. "Stefan can't be part of this."

"I wouldn't want him to be," she said.

Jack said, "I want to meet Zita."

Grace trailed her hand over the tops of vines as they walked. "Once we're certain Gossamer is out of the picture and it's safe, of course."

"Are you going to bring her up here to live with you?"

Grace hesitated. "I want what's best for her."

"That's not an answer."

"I've been so focused on keeping her safe I haven't allowed myself even to dream about it. Does that make me a bad mother?"

Jack watched a cottontail nibbling fresh green shoots of grass circling the base of a support pole. "I'd like it if she lived here. I want her close so I can be part of her life."

"How can you be so sure of that all of a sudden?"

"The same way you were sure when you passed your photos of her to Henri."

She stopped and placed her hand on his arm. "I've always trusted you. I told you that when I saw you at the hospital. I trusted you'd do the right thing in case something bad happened."

"It's not going to. Everything will work out okay as long as we play it cool. Stick to the script, sign the deed over to Gossamer, and then let it hang him."

"But what if it doesn't?"

"It will," he said.

"But you have insurance, right?"

Jack sensed a darkness coming over her, so he reassured her. "It won't come to that. I promise."

"But you have it, right?"

"Let it play out like we wrote it."

Grace started to speak but swallowed her words. She resumed walking. "Bringing Zita here won't be easy. She's been living with Catalina and her family all this time. As far as she knows they're her family."

"Zita will have more family here than she'll know what to do with. You, Stefan. Me and Katie."

"I suppose."

"When you visited her, who did she think you were?"

"She was so young she probably doesn't even remember me. I'd give anything if I could do that all over again. I've made so many mistakes." Grace sighed. "The story of my life and I'm still trying to rewrite it."

"You've kept her safe. That's all that counts."

"But she doesn't have a birth certificate, much less a passport."

"Are you forgetting who we are? Henri will make them."

She hesitated. "I don't know. You sound as if it's all no big deal."

A cloud partially blocked the sun and Jack watched as their shadows melded together. "You know what's a big deal? Coming up with reasons why it can't work. It's the same thing with every con we ever pulled. You spend more time on the what-ifs and the why-nots than you do the actual play. This is going to work."

He looped his arm through hers and turned them around. "Come on. Let's go send Gossamer and Tully on their way to jail."

She leaned into him. "Remember what else I told you at the hospital?"

"Remind me."

"I said you're a confidence man, Jack. Doubt's never been your thing. It's why I fell in love with you."

32

Sunset was still an hour away but already the foothills that boxed Sabbia Plain were suffused with pink and lavender. A crust of alkali formed motionless waves on the dry lakebed. They'd lost their silvery glint in the dying light and were the color of old bones. Even the sheen was off the Citroën's burgundy paint job.

Jack and Grace sat on a picnic blanket spread beside the lifeless lake. There were still a couple of sandwich halves on a plate. The bottle of wine was two glasses short of being full and a bowl of sliced tomatoes mixed with fresh mozzarella and olive oil was nearly empty.

"You're sure they're coming," Grace said.

"They'll be here," he said.

"And the other one?"

"Z-Pak. Tully texted him to get here early to scout it out."

"How do you think Gossamer will take it when he discovers he's been had?"

"Badly, but if all goes right, he'll find that out from the cops."

Jack lifted a pair of binoculars and scanned the horizon.

Grace said, "When you met Katie were you completely over me?"

"You want to talk about that now?"

"It's important."

He exhaled through his nose to keep hot breath from fogging the lenses of the binoculars. "Katie and me? It was a canoe going down a river. It didn't matter if there was a big waterfall ahead or not. It still doesn't."

"What they mean by *real love*," she whispered and sipped some wine. It was her Brunello and stained her umber lips dark. "What will you call your baby?"

Jack thumbed the focus. "We don't know the gender yet."

Grace turned wistful. "I'm sure it will be beautiful. Loved and well-cared for too. Katie's a natural." She finished her wine and put the glass down. "You too. I'm sorry I ever doubted you."

Jack said, "Here they come."

He followed the rooster tail of dust kicked up by the black Lincoln as it turned off the tar and gravel county road and headed down a dirt track toward them. Grace stiffened. Jack put the binoculars down and touched her leg.

"Easy. Let it play out."

Tully exited first. He wore wrap around dark glasses and was dressed in camos and combat boots. He carried a scoped assault rifle. The barrel was angled down but his index finger was trigger ready.

"Who's in your car?" he said.

Jack picked up a sandwich. "See for yourself."

Tully didn't budge. "Where's the big Mex?"

"Mexican American," Jack said.

"Whatever. Where is he?"

"Why don't you call and ask him? I got his number."

Tully raised his gun as he approached the Citroën. He checked the back seat. Then he pushed the dark glasses up on his forehead and scanned the surroundings through the automatic rifle's scope. The plain was flat and treeless. There weren't even rocks big enough for a ground squirrel to find shade behind. The dry lake was as barren as the moon.

"Clear," he said.

Jonathan Gossamer climbed out of the Lincoln. He was carrying a tablet sleeve made of calfskin. The shirt under his blazer was stylishly untucked.

He made a show of taking a deep breath and then crowed. "I do love making money."

"Are we here to make a deal or wax poetic?" Jack said.

Gossamer flicked his tongue at him. "Please search them, Mr. Tully."

Tully ordered them to stand up. He let the automatic rifle swing from its shoulder strap as he patted them down. He found Jack's phone and tossed it aside. Then he booted the wine bottle. A red stain spread across the scrubby ground.

"Hey, that's a gold medal winner. You owe me a hundred bucks," Jack said. He was still holding onto a sandwich and took a bite.

Tully gripped his gun again. "Watch it or I'll spill you."

Jack smiled to himself. "Okay, Gossamer. Let's get this over with before your pit bull here starts humping my leg."

Tully made a move to bash him with the butt of his AR, but Gossamer tut-tutted and cocked his head toward the Lincoln. Tully backed off and went to open the tailgate. He pulled out a folding camp chair and table. He set them up. Gossamer sat down and placed the calfskin sleeve on the table.

"You will appreciate these." He extracted a tablet and tapped the screen. A document appeared. "It is the legal description for the property known as Sabbia Plain, a plot map, a copy of the deed with your LLC listed as the current owner, and a quitclaim."

He seemed pretty pleased with himself. "Have you ever heard of a quitclaim? It is such a useful legal remedy for transferring ownership of a property with the utmost speed. There is no need to conduct a title search nor go through a laborious escrow process."

"Aren't you clever." Jack raised the sandwich in salute but he really meant it for Cicero Broadshank.

"One tries. Since this PDF is DocuSign enabled, all that remains is for you two to sign as grantors and for me to sign as grantee." He handed Jack the tablet.

Jack held onto the sandwich and took his time reading. He sighed deeply and then signed his name with his fingertip. Grace did the same. She handed the tablet back to Gossamer.

He didn't sign right away. A toothy smile spread across his thin face. It gave him the appearance of a weasel about to savor a plump rabbit. "I do enjoy winning. It is so, what is the word, gratifying? No, that is too minimizing of the feeling. Orgasmic. That is much more accurate. A total body and soul orgasm. Ooh, ooh." He made a face, flicked his tongue, and writhed.

Gossamer scribbled the screen with his fingertip and hit save. "Excellent. And I see I have a strong cell signal so why waste time? I can transmit it to the county for recording right now."

"It won't record," Jack said.

Suspicion darkened Gossamer's face. "Why not?"

"When Stefan transferred ownership to the LLC we created, Grace and I had to go down to the recorder's offices and pay a fee. The county always wants its piece of the pie. You'll have to walk it in yourself and write a check."

"You really have been out of the game too long. I do not have to do it in person. I can pay online using electronic transfer. There is a hyperlink form for that attached." Gossamer smirked.

Jack shrugged. "Who knew?"

Gossamer typed in his account information. When he was finished he hit save again and then send. The tablet whooshed.

"Done." He slid it back into the calfskin sleeve. "A word of warning. If there are any irregularities with the deed or its recording, the photographs of poor Ji-min will go straight to the San Francisco Police Department along with your baseball bat." His gaze turned cold as he brought it to bear on Grace. "And I have not forgotten about you either. All it will take is one phone call."

Grace lurched forward but Jack grabbed her arm and held her back. "You got what you wanted, now leave us alone."

"Certainly." Gossamer stood, started to turn toward the Lincoln, and then paused. "No, I think not."

His teeth gleamed. "The story of the blue pearl is quite legendary among our community. A man, a woman, a fake diamond, and a fence who fell victim to his own avarice." Gossamer wagged his finger. "Do not look so surprised. I am hardly a novice nor am I so gullible. I create markets out of thin air and can sell anything to anyone at any time. Even a dry lake." He chuckled and then his mood shifted. "But what I will not do is risk having someone contemplate a double cross or attempt to alert my potential buyers in hopes of a reward for good behavior."

He turned to Tully. "It is time for Mr. Z-Pak to join us. Tell him about the pick and shovel we brought and have him start digging."

Tully fished a phone from the pocket of his camo pants and hit a speed dial. Moments later a new rooster tail of dust rose in the east. Tully tracked its progress through the scope of his AR. Jack kept his grip on Grace's arm.

"Don't do this," he said to Gossamer. "There's no reason to. You got nothing to worry about from us. You have your leverage and can use it whenever you want. You got the deed. You got everything you wanted. You won. Congratulations."

"I know," Gossamer said. "But I want to." And he laughed.

The jacked-up pickup gained ground. Tully kept his eye on the scope.

"Is all in order, Mr. Tully?" Gossamer asked.

Tully turned around. "The light was reflecting off the windshield but I can make him out now."

Gossamer took a few steps back. He surveyed the picnic blanket. "How fitting. And you're still eating a sandwich. The last supper. The blanket will make dragging you to your grave that much easier. Please sit."

Jack said, "Can't we talk about this? You want something else? What? Money? The rights to Grace's water? Name it."

"Stand, sit, fall. It makes no difference to me."

Tully raised the gun at them. The roar of the pickup grew louder.

Jack said. "Hold on. Okay, have it your way. We'll get on the blanket." He guided Grace toward it. "We tried but this one's on them," he whispered.

"I knew it was always going to come to this," she said.

Jack hurled the sandwich. As soon as he did the horn on Z-Pak's truck honked. Tully glanced over. Jack yanked Grace down on the blanket and a rifle shot exploded and then another in rapid succession. Tully flew backwards as the first bullet cleaved his forehead and the second tore through his chest. Gossamer screeched. The pickup skidded to a stop and Eddie jumped from the driver's side as Chaco vaulted from the bed. Both had their pistols drawn, Eddie's pointed at Gossamer and Chaco's at Tully's sprawled corpse.

"Whoa. Hella good shot," Chaco said.

"Both of them," Eddie said. The black ball cap with no logo and orange makeup gave him a jack-o'-lantern appearance.

A ghost rose among the scab of alkali covering the nearby lakebed, its white countenance wavering mirage-like in the fading light. The spirit seemed to hover in place and only took human form as it approached. Hark, wrapped in a shroud of sheets, cradled a scoped long rifle in his arms. He threw the bolt and ejected a spent shell and then kicked the sole of Tully's boot and spit.

"I told you, *cabrone*. I wasn't no FNG."

Jack helped Grace up from the blanket. He looked at Tully and then at Gossamer. "We gave you two choices: walk away or this. You chose poorly."

Gossamer licked his lips. "What are you going to do to me?"

"You say you're a salesman. Start selling."

"Sabbia Plain. I will rescind the quitclaim. The basin is yours. You can run the grift yourself. You will be rich."

"You signed it, you keep it. It's the handcuffs that tie you to fraud according to my lawyer. And he's good. Real good."

Gossamer's eyes started to widen. "Money. I will pay you whatever you want."

Jack picked up his phone from where Tully had tossed it. He called Do Pray, listened, and hung up.

"We already got your money. The moment you hit send with your bank information my guy intercepted it. He's already emptied your accounts."

Gossamer's complexion turned the color of his frosted haircut. "I still have the bat and photographs. Let me go and I will send them to you as soon as I am somewhere safe."

Hark grunted. "What, to an undisclosed location? I heard that bullshit before."

Jack took his time as if thinking about it. "I already got the photos. Your firewall's no good. My guy hacked it as soon as you had a cell signal. The longer you bragged the more time he had to download everything."

"But they are not the only copies," Gossamer said quickly. "I have them on multiple devices."

"Even better because the shots are already on their way to a San Francisco homicide cop. He's got a warrant to search your apartment too. Every device with the photos he finds is another knot in your noose. And, oh yeah, my baseball bat? It's registered for warranty purposes. Has been for years. Got a serial number and everything. The bat behind your washer and dryer? You know how much DNA sloughs off from the inside of a red sneaker?"

Jonathan Gossamer was young but wrinkles were showing in his face as he struggled to find an angle. "So what? It will not prove anyone was murdered because no one is dead. It was all for show."

"You know that, I know that, but Dolan the cop doesn't. One look at those photos and finding the bat, he won't need a body. He'll use it to tie you and Tully to Alison. Rainey's testimony will put you away. Z-Pak's too. He's already in jail by the way. Your friend Carol? A friend who's a wonder calculating odds told her sticking around was a loser. I wouldn't be hoping for a Christmas card if I were you."

Grace clutched Jack. Her fingers dug into his arm, her voice was strained, almost breaking. "Don't forget about Zita. We can't let anybody get to her."

"Not a chance," he said. "Stay cool."

Jack drew up close to Gossamer, so close their chests bumped. "You're going to make a call to Argentina right now and wave off whoever you hired. You'd better hope they answer because if they don't Chaco and Eddie are going to be digging two holes."

Gossamer licked his lips again. "You wouldn't."

"But I would," Hark said and brandished his rifle.

"Don't think. Dial." Jack shoved his phone at him. "Put it on speaker so we can hear."

Gossamer faltered and then started punching in numbers. There was a long pause and then the sound of an international ring tone. Gossamer wheeled abruptly and ran to the Lincoln. He threw open the door and locked it behind him.

He held the phone up. "Anybody moves and I tell them to kill the girl." He started the car.

Grace hammered Jack's shoulder. "Do something!"

Hark had the rifle raised to his shoulder. "He's dead where he sits."

"Hold on," Jack said. "They could be on the phone." He raised his voice. "Gossamer, say the right thing and then you can leave. You have my word."

Gossamer put the phone in the crook of his neck and revved the engine.

"Stop him!" Grace screamed. "He's going to tell them to kill Zita."

"Say the right words or Hark shoots," Jack said.

Grace broke away, reached under the picnic blanket, and pulled out the Lady Hawk 9mm she'd hidden there. She charged the Lincoln, the gun held straight out with both hands. Gossamer threw the crossover in gear and stamped the accelerator. Grace squeezed the trigger. She kept squeezing it. The windshield spidered from multiple rounds and then the bumper struck her. She went down and under and the heavy car with a deadman's red Puma pressed on the gas dragged her across the plain.

Jack didn't even know he was running as he chased after the dust cloud. His chest heaved, his heart pounded, and his ears rang with his own cries. The car finally let go and he skidded on his knees beside her. She lay on her back. Her body was bent at an angle that defied anatomical geometry. Blood darkened her wine-stained lips, and the blue in her eyes was already softer than the color of the dusking sky.

Jack stared into them and saw the first time they met, the kiss at Coit Tower, the days and nights in a hotel suite making love, the clink of champagne glasses as they celebrated the score from the blue pearl. He could lie to her and say everything was going to be all right. He could tell her the truth and say he would've grabbed for her when she tumbled from the edge of the razor blade they danced upon if only given the chance. But neither was what she wanted or needed to hear.

He put his lips to her ear. "I'll get Zita and she'll always know you were a good mother and loved her. She'll never forget you. Neither will I."

Jack kissed her good-bye as the light went out in her eyes and her last breath flew away on the hushed wings of a dove.

33

El Niño roared back with a vengeance. King tides pushed San Francisco Bay over the top of the Embarcadero and flooded Alviso. Gully washers rushed down gutters and carried away cars torn free from their parking brakes. Hipsters exchanged skateboards for skimboards and hurled themselves down the crooked twists and turns of Lombard Street. Bars never poured so many Irish coffees.

The homeless encampment moved back to San Francisco General Hospital. The air was thick and feral from their funk, but Jack's mind was on anything but opossums as he pushed his way through the crowded cafeteria and made his way to the elevator bank.

He got off on the fourth floor and entered Henri LeConte's room. Katie was sitting by his bedside, Chagall curled at her feet. She jumped up and threw her arms around him.

"I missed you," she said. "Are you okay?"

"I'll do," Jack said.

"I'm sorry about Grace," she said.

"Me too."

He reached over and touched Henri's shoulder. "I tried."

The old forger gave an empathetic nod. His hair was combed, his pencil thin moustache neatly trimmed, a colorful silk ascot tied around his neck.

They stood in silence for a while and then Katie said, "Henri's made a lot of progress since they took the ventilator out. Show Jack. Say hello."

Henri struggled for a moment and then the words came haltingly. *"Bonjour, mon fils."*

"Isn't it amazing," Katie said. "They've been giving him speech therapy but the only thing he remembers is French. It's like someone who got chemo. They go in with straight hair and afterward it grows back curly."

Henri gave a Gallic shrug.

Katie said, "Is it all over now?"

Jack told them how Deputy Florencia Santos filed charges against Z-Pak and transferred him to the county jail in Stockton. News about Terry Dolan solving Alison's murder and Ji-min's disappearance after both suspects were found to have apparently killed each other in a shootout was spreading across the Internet.

"I spoke to Stefan this morning," Jack said. "The county gave him permission to bury Grace on the vineyard."

"She'd like that," Katie said.

The door opened and Taylor S. clomped in, her clogs a drumbeat on the waxed floor. "Why the gloom, handsome? You're not getting nervous on me with this baby about to come are you?"

"But she's not due for another couple of weeks." Jack squinted at Katie. "Isn't that right?"

She tapped the corner of her eye. "Taylor thinks otherwise, and who am I to question a woman's intuition."

"Right," Jack said.

"Right what?" Katie lobbed back.

"Nothing," he said.

"When you say nothing you mean something. What are you planning?"

Jack peered out the hospital room window. A veil of rain blocked the view of his boyhood neighborhood in the Mission District.

"I bought a ticket to Argentina for tonight."

"Argentina?" Taylor S. said. "This is no time for a vacation."

"It's not a vacation," Katie said. "He's going to get his daughter."

"What daughter?" the nurse said.

"Zita," Katie said.

Jack put up his hand. "I can wait."

"But *she* can't." Katie said.

"But what about our baby?"

"What about it?"

"Taylor said you could go into labor any minute."

"So what? Need I remind you about the Mahicans? The women would go down to the riverside and give birth alone. Bantu women deliver in a mud hut accompanied only by an elder female."

Taylor S. cocked her hip and patted her bouffant. "Who you calling elder?"

Katie winked at her and then said, "Besides, I spend most of my time here visiting Henri anyway. What better place to be if my water breaks? Zita is your *'das-pa*, *da-tla-ba*, and *ma-'ong-ba* and you're hers." She cupped her palms under her protruding belly. "Ours too. Go bring this baby's big sister home."

Jack didn't have to be told twice. After everything that happened he knew past, present, and future could never be denied. He also didn't wait for the elevator. He was down the stairs, across the lobby, and reached the front doors so fast no one had time to panhandle him. He ran straight into Hark.

"What's with the flowers?" Jack asked.

Hark looked at the bouquet as if somehow the dozen red roses had magically bloomed in his hands.

"They for Henri?"

Hark shook his head.

"Katie?"

Again a shake and then a sheepish grin crossed his face.

"I get it. Well, Taylor S. is one helluva woman. Good luck with that." Jack started moving again.

Hark said, "Where's the fire?"

"I got a plane to catch."

"Where to?"

"Buenos Aires. I'm going to find Zita."

"But you don't even got an address. And what about those dudes Goss hired?"

"If they're still hanging around, I'll deal with them. You can bet the *estancia* on it. Catch you later."

Jack pulled up his collar and as he stepped into the hard rain Hark called after him.

"Wait up, *'mano*. If there's going be a tango count me in."

And he shoved the bouquet into the hands of a homeless woman shuffling by and moved fast for a big man.

A NOTE FROM THE AUTHOR

Thank you so much for reading *BABY BLUE*. I'd truly appreciate it if you would please leave a review on Amazon and Goodreads. Your feedback not only helps me become a better storyteller, but you help other readers by blazing a trail and leaving markers for them to follow as they search for new stories.

To leave a review, go to the *BABY BLUE* product page on Amazon, click "customer reviews" next to the stars below the title, click the "Write a customer review" button, and share your thoughts with other readers.

To quote John Cheever, "I can't write without a reader. It's precisely like a kiss—you can't do it alone."

GET A FREE BOOK

Dwight Holing's genre-spanning work includes novels, short fiction, and nonfiction. His mystery and suspense thriller series include The Nick Drake Novels and The Jack McCoul Capers. The stories in his collections of literary short fiction have won awards, including the Arts & Letters Prize for Fiction. He has written and edited numerous nonfiction books on nature travel and conservation. He is married to a kick-ass environmental advocate; they have a daughter and son, and two dogs who'd rather swim than walk.

Sign up for his newsletter to get a free book and be the first to learn about his next novel as well as receive news about crime fiction and special deals.

Visit dwightholing.com/free-book. You can unsubscribe at any time.

ALSO BY DWIGHT HOLING

The Nick Drake Novels

The Sorrow Hand (Book 1)

The Pity Heart (Book 2)

The Shaming Eyes (Book 3)

The Whisper Soul (Book 4)

The Jack McCoul Capers

A Boatload (Book 1)

Bad Karma (Book 2)

Baby Blue (Book 3)

Shake City (Book 4)

Short Story Collections

California Works

Over Our Heads Under Our Feet